THE TINY HERO
of Ferny Creek Library

THE TINY HERO

of Ferny Creek Library

By **Linda Bailey**

Pictures by
Victoria Jamieson

GREENWILLOW BOOKS
An Imprint of HarperCollins*Publishers*

This book is a work of fiction. References to real people, events, establishments, organizations, or locales are intended only to provide a sense of authenticity, and are used to advance the fictional narrative. All other characters, and all incidents and dialogue, are drawn from the author's imagination and are not to be construed as real.

The Tiny Hero of Ferny Creek Library
Text copyright © 2017 by Linda Bailey
Illustrations copyright © 2017 by Victoria Jamieson

The text of this book is set in 13-point Century Schoolbook.
Book design by Paul Zakris

Library of Congress Cataloging-in-Publication Data is available.
ISBN 978-0-06-244093-8 (hardcover)
18 19 20 21 CG/LSCH 10 9 8 7 6 5 4 3 2

Greenwillow Books
An Imprint of HarperCollinsPublishers

To teacher-librarians and children's librarians everywhere,
who bring kids and books together . . .
and change lives!

CHAPTER
1

"I knew this would happen," said Ma. "I told her and told her—stop reading! It's dangerous! Didn't I *say* that?"

"Of course you did," said Pa. "But you know what Min's like. She does what she wants."

Eddie crouched behind a piece of yellow chalk, listening. He'd been asking his parents about Aunt Min ever since last Tuesday, when she didn't come home from the Library. But his mother had brushed off his questions.

"Stop worrying," she kept saying. "Your aunt can look after herself."

But now, here it was—the truth. Ma was worried, too.

"What are we going to do?" she asked, her voice rising to a squeak.

There was a long pause.

Eddie, just steps away, ducked even lower behind the chalk. He knew his parents were trying to have a private conversation. With so many children in the family, the only way they could be alone was to leave their home behind the chalkboard and sit out on the ledge. They spoke in hushed tones—the way your parents might whisper on a balcony if they didn't want you to hear.

"There's only one way," said Pa slowly. "I'll

have to go look for her."

"You?" said Ma. "With *your* legs? You certainly will not. You'd never make it past the door."

Eddie peered at the classroom door. From this distance, it was mostly a blur. But he knew it was a very long walk. And Ma was right—Pa's back legs were so creaky, he could barely crawl down to the floor.

"I have to," said Pa. "Min may be hurt. She may be—"

"Don't say it!" said Ma. "Oh, I could just spit. There was no need for any of this. She could have stayed home, snug as a bug in a rug. Plenty of books right here in this classroom. But no, she had to go to the *Library*! She had to risk her life—and now she's risking yours, too. All because of this foolish, unnatural habit. I ask you—what does a bug need with reading?"

Pa let out a sigh. "Well, I don't understand it myself, but ever since we came here—"

"Don't you go defending her," said Ma. "She's corrupted Eddie, too. Every chance he gets, creeping into some book. It's like he's *trying* to get killed! I tell you, it's a weakness in your family, this book reading. A terrible flaw. Look what happened to your father."

Now it was Eddie who let out a sigh. He'd heard this sad tale so often, he could say it by heart. Grandpa George had suffered a Tragic Death on page 131 of *The Wonderful Wizard of Oz* when some unthinking child had slammed the book shut. Poor Grandpa George, thought Eddie. He had died without ever knowing what happened to Dorothy.

Ma, meanwhile, wasn't finished. "It's out of the question," she told Pa. "*You* can't go after Min. It'll have to be *me*."

"Now, wait," said Pa, "that's not right. What about the babies?"

Ma didn't answer. What could she say? There were twenty-seven grubs tucked away in the wall, depending on her care.

"Well, then," she muttered. "Who?"

There was a long pause.

"What about . . . Eddie?" said Pa.

Eddie couldn't help himself—he jumped. Stumbling sideways, he fell against the chalk, which started to roll. He grabbed it before Ma could see.

But she was far too upset to notice.

"Eddie?" squawked Ma. "Have you lost your mind? *Eddie?* I love our Eddie to bits, but we both know the truth. He's a dreamer, a fool—a nincompoop! He can hardly find his way off this chalkboard. No way, no chance, no how is my baby boy wandering off through this huge endless school to hunt for a crazy old bug who should have known better."

"Hush," said Pa. Then he sighed. "You're right, of course. This is too tough for Eddie."

"Darn tootin'!" said Ma. "And besides, he stands out. Bright color like that, it's just asking for trouble. You know he shouldn't be out in the open."

They both went quiet. Thinking.

The problem was—and Eddie knew it—there

was no one else to think of. Just their own family.

Oh, they had plenty of friends and relatives out in the Big Woods. But only Eddie and his closest family had had the bad luck to get scooped up one evening and dropped into a glass tank of dirt in Room 19 of Ferny Creek Elementary School. For two weeks, they had been a fourth-grade science project. And then came the fateful night when the Cleaner knocked over the tank, dirt and all. He was only gone a few minutes to fetch a shovel. But while he was gone, the bugs saw their chance. . . .

And that was the *other* big story Eddie had heard his whole life. The Great Escape. How Grandma Ruth had bravely led the family away from the tank, across the huge classroom, and up the wall. How she had managed, with her unerring sense of direction, to sniff out the crack behind the chalkboard that they now called home.

But now Grandma Ruth was gone. So was Grandpa George. There were only Eddie and his parents left, and his fifty-three younger brothers and sisters.

And Aunt Min, of course.

Was she all right?

Was she alive?

In his entire life, Eddie couldn't remember a single time that Aunt Min hadn't come home.

Someone would have to go after her.

Eddie stared at the big blurry door.

CHAPTER 2

Sunrise was Eddie's best chance. He couldn't sneak away at night when his parents were awake. He couldn't travel in broad daylight, either. The school was much too dangerous then.

No, the best time to leave was dawn—right after his family fell asleep, and before the Squishers arrived.

Early the next morning, when the first pale light stole through the classroom windows, he was ready.

As his family settled down for their morning nap, Eddie pretended to join them. He claimed a spot near the exit—that fortunate crack in the wall, behind the oh-so-lucky gap in the chalkboard, that together and almost miraculously allowed the bugs to come and go. Eddie huddled there quietly as the new babies curled and twisted. He watched as his younger brothers and sisters had a last roll and wrestle. He waited as Ma and Pa sank into a sleepy torpor that could be disturbed only by something loud or bright.

Eddie was not about to give them either. Moving just his eyes, he gazed slowly around at the crumbling plaster. Finally, when all was quiet, he rose onto all six feet.

As he crept toward the exit, a voice rang out.

"Eddie? Hey, EDDIE! Where you GOING?"

A small dark head popped up among his siblings. Alfie!

Eddie groaned. Of all the brothers and sisters who might have spotted him . . .

"Can I COME, TOO?"

"Shh!" hissed Eddie. For reasons that no one understood, Alfie had been hatched with a powerful voice. It came and went in odd bursts.

"Alfie, quiet!" whispered Eddie, glancing at their sleeping parents. "I just have . . . a . . . you know, a thing I have to do."

"WHAT thing?"

"It's a secret. I can't tell you."

"Aww, come on," Alfie whined. "Just TELL ME, okay? I won't tell anyone else. PLEEEEAASE?"

Eddie wanted nothing more than to leap on his little brother and clamp those mandibles shut. But there were too many bugs in the way.

"Okay," he said quickly. "I'm going to the Library to find Aunt Min. But you can't come, Alfie, and you can't tell anyone. Promise?"

"Aww," said Alfie. "Why can't I come? WHYYYYYY?"

"Go to sleep!" ordered Eddie. "Now!"

And before his little brother could blurt one more word, Eddie slipped through the exit.

Out on the ledge, he paused, antennae quivering. The classroom was cool and fresh at this time of day. The desks were still neatly arranged. Eddie gazed at the familiar art on the walls. He stared at the large whiteboards where the Teacher liked to write things down—a *very* good choice for the bugs, as it happened, as it left the old gray chalkboard to them.

Eddie waited on the ledge now till he was sure it was safe. Then he beetled to the end of the chalkboard, dodging around chalk stubs and climbing over erasers. He knew all the places where chalk dust collected and stepped carefully around the mounds.

At the end of the ledge, a large bulletin board was attached to the wall. It had a sturdy wood frame and was safer to climb down than the wall—still slippery from a new paint job. Eddie scrambled down the frame and dropped smoothly to the floor.

So far, so good. There was the huge metal desk

that belonged to the Teacher. His name was Mr. Patullo, and he was a pleasant, friendly man—except, of course, for the fact that he had bug-napped Eddie's entire family. (Ma would *never* forgive him for that.)

Eddie gazed longingly at the Teacher's desk. Was there a book left open on top? Sometimes there was. If he climbed up to check . . .

Then he noticed what he was doing.

Daydreaming.

Already.

"Concentrate!" he told himself, turning to the distant gray doorway.

It was terrifying and wonderful, all at once. Through that portal, somewhere to the north and miraculously reachable by even a small bug, was . . . the Library!

If you want the whole truth about Eddie, here it is. Yes, he was worried about Aunt Min. Yes, he was the only one who could search for her. But also, with every bit of his itty-bitty being, Eddie longed to travel to . . . the *Library*!

Grandpa George had visited the Library dozens of times. He'd always come home dazzled. Grandpa George was the one who had figured out how to read in the first place—teaching himself slowly, letter by letter, never giving up, not even with the q's and x's. Then he'd taught Aunt Min to read and took her to the Library with him. Aunt Min had, in turn, taught Eddie. She'd tried with his sisters and brothers, too, but they weren't interested. The only *young* book bug in the family was Eddie. The Library had become his great dream.

And now here he was. On his way!

He set off across the great expanse of brown linoleum, speckled with bright colors. Eddie was fond of those speckles. They provided great camouflage for a bug of any color.

He passed a desk. He passed chairs with green legs and rubber feet. Another desk, another chair. When he reached the orange carpet, he had already ventured farther than he'd ever been from home.

The carpet looked peculiar, up close. Thick.

Fluffy. Eddie gave it a nervous poke with his antennae. Soft, as Pa had said. Not good for walking on.

"Your feet sink in," Pa had warned. "Stay away from carpets!"

Remembering this, Eddie walked carefully around it. More desks, more chairs. This was taking longer than expected.

"Faster!" he told himself.

When at last he reached the doorway, he discovered—bonus!—a raisin, tucked into a corner of the door frame. How had the Cleaner missed *that*? Just when Eddie was getting hungry, too. It was as if it were waiting for him.

He took a chaw. The raisin was dusty, but delicious. As Eddie enjoyed his surprise snack, he felt almost cheerful.

Can't be far to the Library now, he thought.

Pushing his raisin ahead of him, he stepped through the classroom door.

"Oh . . . my . . . gosh!" whispered Eddie, and he leaned on the raisin for support.

CHAPTER
3

Eddie's eyes bugged out as he stared at the great school hallway. Never had he seen anything like it!

How could he have? When his family moved into Ferny Creek Elementary, he had been a very young bug. He couldn't remember the Big Woods at all, and except for short jaunts in the classroom, he had spent his whole life behind a chalkboard.

What he saw now was a shock.

"Where does it end?" he wondered, gazing around. Above him, nothing but space, fading into infinity. To the left, a vast soaring tunnel that went on and on, disappearing into a square of hazy light. He turned to the right. Another lofty tunnel. More nothingness.

Eddie sank slowly to the floor. At least the floor was still there, solid and reliable. He lay flat on its surface, trying to gather his courage, which seemed to have rolled right out of him onto the long wooden floorboards.

"Don't panic," he told himself. "Grandpa George did it. So did Aunt Min."

Aunt Min! Suddenly he missed her terribly. They were supposed to do this together. She had promised to *take* him to the Library. "When you're old enough," she always said.

Was he old enough now?

Was he?

Looking around, he was struck by another thought. Aunt Min had talked about the hallway. She said it led to the Library—and yes, that it was like a tunnel. But she'd never mentioned that it went in two different directions.

Which way should he go?

"To the north," Aunt Min had said. Where was "north"?

Letting out a whimper, he sank even flatter.

Time passed. Eddie couldn't have told you how much time, but it was enough to realize that he couldn't just lie there, flopped like a worm on the floor.

He forced himself to stand. Then he forced himself to think. He remembered something else Aunt Min had said: "The moment I get through the classroom door, I can *smell* the Library."

Smell! Eddie was good at smells. But what did the Library smell like? It took only a second to figure it out. Books, of course. Eddie knew what a book smelled like.

He wiggled his antennae, trying to pick up a scent. First left. Then right.

Left! It definitely smelled more booky.

One step at a time. That was how to get there. Or rather, *three* steps at a time. Like other six-leggers, Eddie moved three legs forward when he walked—front and back on one side, and middle leg on the other.

Staying close to the wall, he set out.

He glanced back at his raisin. A shame to leave it. But it would slow him down, and he had wasted enough time already. A thin yellow light washed over the end of the hallway ahead. It wouldn't be long. . . .

He trekked on. One foot after another. After another. After another. After another. After another.

It wasn't working. He was too slow. His legs had never walked this far. They were starting to tremble.

Eddie had his head down, concentrating, when he heard a loud sound.

CLANG!

He recognized it immediately. He heard it every morning. It meant that the big front door of the school had just opened and slammed shut, letting in—a Squisher!

Oh no, thought Eddie. So soon?

A tall shape, like a moving tower, came marching down the hall. Eddie scampered to the wall and shrank against its baseboard. As the shape got closer, he saw that it was an adult Squisher, carrying an armload of folders. She swooshed right past him without slowing.

Eddie stared at the baseboard. It ran all along the bottom of the hallway wall, and when he noticed the color, his heart sank.

White.

He looked down at his body. Green. But not just *any* green. Eddie's exoskeleton was the kind of bright, vibrant green that stood out against a white baseboard like an emerald on snow.

This is bad, he thought.

The door CLANGED again.

Eddie's mind raced. He wasn't going to reach the Library in time—that much was clear—and the great flood of Squishers was about to come rushing in, as it did every morning. Soon the hall would be thick with them.

Somewhere to hide, he thought. Just till it's over.

He scurried along the baseboard, searching

wildly. A crack? A hole?

Nothing but smooth white wood.

The front door was opening regularly now—*CLANG! CLANG! CLANG!* There were voices, young and old, and a great roaring *THUD, THUD, THUD* as feet went thundering past. The floorboards shook.

Oh no, thought Eddie. No!

He scuttled faster. Wasn't there a tiny crack *anywhere*?

As the hallway grew more crowded, the danger rose. The Squishers couldn't *all* walk down the middle. Some had to walk on the sides. Close to the walls. Close to Eddie! The closer they came, the more frightened he got.

An enormous blue running shoe slammed down—*WHAM!*—right next to him, so close he could have touched it.

That did it.

For one brief panicky moment, Eddie tried to run in every direction at once. Then he jammed himself against the baseboard, pulled in his

head and legs, and froze. If he was going to get squished, it would happen right here. He waited . . . expecting at any second . . . the giant crushing foot!

Instead the *THUD*s faded.

The hall grew quiet.

Eddie took a breath. He stepped slowly away from the wall.

CLANG!

A last, late Squisher. A young one, racing down the hall. *THUD! THUD! THUD!* She was almost past Eddie when—*CRASH!*—an untied shoelace took her down, along with her bag full of stuff. Pencils, notebook, sandwich went flying. A hard, flat object skittered across the floor and settled beside Eddie.

He stared.

A book.

It had fallen *open*.

"Don't!" he told himself.

But he couldn't hold back. He darted to the book. Scrambling onto the open pages, he raced across these words, reading as he ran:

roared their terrible roars

and gnashed their terrible teeth

Oh my gosh! Eddie *knew* this story. *Where the Wild Things Are*! Aunt Min could tell it from memory. It was a brilliant story.

Then he remembered.

Looked up.

Gasped.

The Squisher was *right there*! Kneeling on her great, colossal knees. Snatching up her belongings.

I'm done for, thought Eddie. He couldn't believe his own foolishness. Here he was, facing certain death—and trying to read a *book*!

"Oh, Ma," he thought. "You're right. I *am* a nincompoop."

But Ma would never know she was right. Because looming above Eddie, staring straight down, was—the Squisher!

"Ick!" said the Squisher. "A bug."

The last words I'll ever hear, thought Eddie.

He wished he had eyelids, so he could close them. He waited for it. The Big Squish. Would she take her shoe off to do it? Use her fist? Or would he end up like Grandpa George, squashed between the pages of a book?

He waited.

And waited.

"Hmm," said the Squisher. "Go on, little greenie. Go home."

Instead of a shoe, a huge finger came down. Flick! Eddie tumbled onto the floor. The book disappeared.

So did the Squisher. *THUD. THUD. THUD.*

Eddie was alone, the Squisher's words still ringing in his ears.

Go home?

Suddenly he wished he could. He wished it more than anything.

CHAPTER
4

If you have ever lived through a terrible disaster—a tornado, perhaps, or a hurricane, or a fiery, plunging meteorite—then you will know how Eddie felt as the Squisher walked away.

He stumbled to the wall and slumped against it. His legs shook so badly that, gazing down, he could actually *see* the fear rippling through them.

The word *home* echoed in his head.

Should he go back? The Squishers were busy in their classrooms now. If he walked quickly, he could get back to Room 19 before the next bell. He could hide behind the door till everyone left.

Yes, that was what he should do. Home was safe. It was cozy and warm and smelled pleasantly buggy. Looking down, he saw that his feet were already moving in that direction. Should he listen to his feet?

"Go home," they seemed to say. "What are you thinking, rushing off like this? *You* don't know how to rescue anyone."

He was standing there wavering when a new thought struck—so sad and so scary, it made his whole being ache.

Aunt Min.

What if she never came back?

She was his teacher. His first, best, and only. If it weren't for Min, Eddie would know nothing of life—nothing except a small, crowded crack-in-a-wall. It was Aunt Min who had told Eddie stories about the Great Worlds Beyond. Amazing, mysterious places. One of them, you had to fly to. It was called Neverland. Another, at the end of a yellow brick road, was known as Oz. There was a magical school, too—called Hogwarts. And if you happened to fall down a rabbit hole, you might end up in a place called Wonderland, where if you ate a magic cake, you would grow huge.

How Eddie would have *loved* to find that cake. For a moment, he let himself dream. . . .

He came to with a start. And in that instant, looking around the hallway—at its towering height, its endless length, its echoing depth—he had a flash of understanding.

He, Eddie, was in a Great World Beyond! He *too* was on a journey. Like Peter and Dorothy and Harry and Alice in the stories, he was traveling to a mysterious, magical place.

He couldn't turn back. Did Dorothy turn back? Peter? Harry? Alice? Never! Nor would Eddie. However small, green, and useless he was, he had to try.

"Follow the yellow brick road," he said out loud, remembering Dorothy. Eddie's road wasn't made of bricks, of course, but the wooden floorboards were yellow. It wasn't hard to pretend.

"Follow the yellow brick road," he said even louder. And with the sound of his own voice and a road like *that* to follow, Eddie and his feet felt just a bit braver.

The scariest part was the doorways.

Each time he came to one, he peered inside, hoping to see the Library. Each time, he found a classroom instead.

The doorways were wide. They forced Eddie to leave the safety of the wall and step into the open. Nowhere to hide. Each time he reached a doorway, he had to *force* himself across.

There was only one way. Run! Just hope with all his heart it would be okay—and run, run, no stopping! Run!

Three great gaping doorways in all. He crossed them at lightning speed.

The fourth door was smaller and closed. Eddie could see black letters on it. Excited, he gazed up.

BOYS

Eddie read the word. Then he read it again, surprised. It was like a door in storybook, he thought. You open a door that says "Treasure," and inside you find treasure. Heaps of it. You open a door that says "Boys," and inside . . .

He was so enjoying this thought that he stopped paying attention.

Suddenly, his antennae buzzed wildly. He turned.

Legs!

Long, bendy, impossibly thin. Creeping along the baseboard.

He looked up and almost fainted. That thing had *way* too many eyes! And in the second that he realized what the thing was—a spider—he also realized what he must look like through those eyes.

Food!

Eddie fled. Back he raced—to his parents, to the classroom. Away from the spider, bearing down now at a shocking rate. He ran for his life, even knowing it was hopeless. The spider was bigger. It was stronger. It had two extra legs!

At that moment, *eeeerrrk*. A door opened.

Eddie turned. It was the door that said "Boys."

And there in the doorway, just like in a story-book, was—a boy.

"Hey!" said the boy, bending down. "Spider. Cool!"

The spider stopped faster than Eddie would have believed possible. It turned and ran—in the opposite direction.

"Don't go," said the boy. "I won't hurt you."

Eddie watched as the boy followed the spider down the hall. The boy looked interested, that's all. He hunched over as he walked, watching the spider and showing no inclination to squish. Eddie waited till they disappeared. Then, with a last little shudder, he moved on.

Soon he came across another door with black letters.

GIRLS

He stared for a while, thinking about the girls behind the door. As he walked away, he let himself hope that there would be a third door that said "Bugs." But of course there wasn't.

"Follow the yellow brick road," he told himself

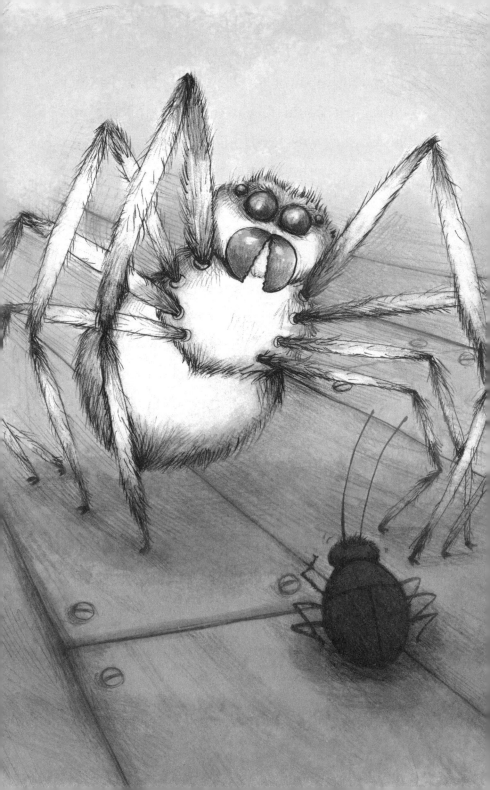

again, trotting ever more quickly along the floor-boards. He could feel a tingle in the air now. The Library was starting to become real. It was just ahead, he was sure. He could smell it more clearly with every step.

And when he finally arrived . . .

He knew it in an instant.

Gazing into the room, he felt a jolt of recognition, even though he'd never been there before. Maybe it was the gentle hush in the air. Or the glorious, fusty smell of hundreds of books in one place. The paper. The ink. The stories. Oh, the stories! He stood there, breathing it in. He had smelled books before, of course. But never so many at once.

The Library was just as he had dreamed. Just as Aunt Min had described. The shelves rose like friendly castle walls, each with its rows of treasures. There was the story-time carpet, spread softly in welcome, waiting for young Squishers to gather. Over there was the comfy couch, offering its own invitation—sit down, curl up, enjoy. And there in the corner was a large rocking chair, brightly painted in many different colors. Eddie knew it immediately. It was the story-time chair where the Librarian read aloud in her rich, lilting voice. Eddie had never heard that voice, of course, but he knew all about it. Aunt Min said it was as sweet as a chocolate chip.

And just as Eddie was having that thought, he *heard* it. The Librarian's voice. It was coming from the bookshelves.

"Are you looking for information on wolves, Jasper? That will be in nonfiction. Let's look together."

Eddie's antennae quivered. Bliss! If the Librarian sounded this wonderful just talking, how must she sound reading a story? He could have listened to her all day.

He could have stood in that doorway all day, too . . . if it weren't so dangerous. Sunshine poured through a skylight in the Library ceiling, flooding the whole entrance with light. Eddie glanced up. Dappled treetops. Plump white clouds.

Min *loved* that skylight.

Nervously he crept forward, checking for danger. The cream-colored linoleum on the Library floor was pleasant to walk on, but it made him stand out like a freshly picked pea. Plus there were young Squishers everywhere! The Librarian had just spoken to one, and Eddie could hear others roaming about.

Where was Aunt Min?

On the left side of the doorway, he could see the Librarian's huge oak desk. Aunt Min said it was a "treasure" that had been there since the school was first built. Eddie paused to admire its rich golden wood. It stood away from the wall with a chair behind it where the Librarian could sit to greet children.

Beyond the desk was a counter and then round tables with chairs. Along the wall was a row of desks, each with its own computer. There was also a large white screen.

On the right side of the Library, beyond the Story Time area and bookshelves, huge windows looked out at the Ferny Creek woods, where Eddie had been born.

And far away, at the very end of the Library, stood a tall wooden cabinet. It was beautifully carved and painted red with bright decorative trim—blue, green, yellow. Eddie couldn't see it clearly, but he knew it well. It was Min's favorite bookshelf in the whole Library.

Might she be *there*?

It was worth a try. He turned left, planning to creep along the wall for safety. He knew, from Aunt Min, that the Librarian was different from most Squishers. She was friendly to ants and flies and moths, and even shooed mosquitoes out the window. But the young Squishers? Unpredictable! You just never knew what a young Squisher would do. Eddie's antennae trembled as he crept forward.

The wall took Eddie behind the Librarian's desk and behind the back of her chair—a cushy-looking green chair with tiny round wheels on the bottom. Eddie had never seen a chair with wheels before. He wondered if the Librarian went riding on it. A picture came into his head of the Librarian riding her chair down the hallway at night.

"Wheee!" she shouted.

The thought made him laugh—a sharp bark of mirth. He choked back the sound immediately. Had the Squishers heard?

No, it didn't seem so. He started to move on.

But wait! What was that? Something strange, yet familiar. A sound so small and faint, he strained his whole body to listen.

"Eddie," he heard.

Imagined?

"Eddie."

He looked around.

"Hello?" he said.

"Up here, Eddie! Look up."

CHAPTER
5

Eddie gazed up, searching the Librarian's chair and desk.

There! On the top of the desk, at the edge. A tiny dot. And sticking out—were those antennae?

"Aunt Min? Oh Auntie Min, is that you?"

"Eddie, shh! Not so loud."

"Everyone's so worried!" he cried. "Why haven't you come home?"

"Hush, Eddie! Scoot up here. Quickly."

Eddie was about to ask *her* to come down, where it was safer. But she had already disappeared. He had no choice but to start climbing the closest leg of the wooden desk. There were plenty of grooves and bumps to grip onto. Still, it wasn't easy after his long, exhausting hike.

He hauled himself onto the desktop, feeling confused. Why couldn't Aunt Min have scooted down?

Then he saw why. Two of her legs—middle-left and back-right—were bent in unusual ways as she balanced on the other four.

"Aunt Min, you're hurt!"

"Just a couple of small breaks, dear. Oh, I am *so* glad to see you!" She gave Eddie a hug.

It wasn't her usual hug. Not at all. And when she pulled away, Eddie could see how thin she was. Aunt Min had never been a big bug, but now she looked shrunken. Old. Wispy enough to be blown away by a breeze.

"How are your parents?" she asked in a rush. "And the little ones? Bobby? Ricky? Jenny? Milly, Billy, Margie, Lily, Mattie, Joey, Gerry, Rosie, Deb—"

"Fine!" said Eddie. "Everyone's fine. What about you, Aunt Min? What are you doing *here*? On a desk? In broad daylight?"

He glanced around nervously. The far end of the desk was cluttered with mysterious objects, but here the desktop was open and exposed—in a room full of roving Squishers. Aunt Min could hardly have picked a more dangerous location.

"No choice," she said. "I had an accident last Tuesday. Ever since then, I've been trapped here. I tried to climb down, but I can't."

"Oh, Aunt Min."

"No use fretting," said Min, but she too looked worried as she glanced around. "We can't stay here. Follow me."

He watched her stagger away, slow and

unsteady. Each step required a great lurch from side to side. Eddie's heart sank.

"Here!" she said. "My hideaway."

Eddie stared at the two desk trays, one stacked above the other. The top tray was supported by four corner posts. The bottom held a sloppy stack of papers.

"Home sweet home," said Aunt Min, heaving herself into the bottom tray. She squeezed into a space between the side of the tray and the papers. Eddie followed.

"You see?" she said. "Could be worse."

"Not *much* worse," said Eddie, looking around.

The living space was sliver thin. Eddie wasn't used to a lot of space, of course. But this felt cramped, even for a bug. And that wasn't the worst part.

"It's not safe," he said. "You know it's not. What if the Librarian moves these papers?"

"She won't. Have a look. They've been here since the first cockroaches walked the globe."

Eddie peered at the papers. The edges were

curled. A thin coat of dust lay on top.

"We're safe," said Min, "for now, anyway."

Suddenly she turned, her whole body trembling. "Oh, Eddie, I'm so desperately hungry. I don't suppose you brought any food?"

Eddie remembered the raisin. "Oh! Sorry, no. You mean . . . you haven't eaten? In all this time?"

"Not really. Just a little apple juice the Librarian spilled the other day. The problem is, she eats all her food at the couch these days. If only I could get to that couch, I know I'd find something."

Eddie said the only thing he could.

"I'll do it," he promised. "I'll go!"

Min gave him a searching look. "Really? You think you can make it?"

He thought hard. Getting to the couch was one thing. But could he carry back food? He stared at his aunt. So shaky. So frail.

So hungry!

"Absolutely," he told her.

"I don't know," muttered Min. "It's so *risky* at this hour. Especially for a bright little guy like you." She gestured at Eddie's green body. She, too, had a greenish tint—but much darker, so she looked almost black. In Eddie's whole family, he was the only truly colorful bug.

"You're starving," said Eddie simply.

Min nodded. "If I don't get a meal in me soon, I'll probably eat *you!*"

Eddie took a step back.

She let out a weak laugh. "Kidding, Eddie, kidding. Okay, if you're really willing to try, here's what you do. Hide under the desk till the recess bell rings. Wait for the children to leave. Then run, quick as you can, to the couch and look underneath."

"Got it," said Eddie, smiling at the word *children*. Aunt Min was the only bug he knew who called them that. "I'm fond of children," she sometimes said. "From a distance, of course. If you listen to them talk, they can be quite amusing."

Remembering this, Eddie chose his words carefully. "I'll wait till the *children* leave."

"Good. Now listen closely. You *must* be back before the next bell rings. Understand?"

Eddie nodded. He knew, from growing up in Room 19, how the school bells worked. The first recess bell would send the children outdoors. The next would bring them thundering back, smelling of grass and fresh air.

Min stared at him, fondness and fear in her eyes. "Dear book bug Eddie," she said. "I shouldn't be asking this of you. Your mother would be horrified. And speaking of your mother, I'm surprised she let you come."

Eddie felt a stab of guilt. He wondered if his mother was still asleep. When she woke up, she *would* be horrified. He remembered the words she had used to describe him.

Dreamer. Fool. Nincompoop.

For a second, he sagged.

Then he rose again to his full height. "Auntie Min, if I'm as hopeless as everyone thinks, how do you suppose I got *here*?"

Min cocked her head, then cackled. "Well,

that's true, isn't it? How *did* you get here? I don't remember giving you directions. And your parents certainly don't know the way."

"I'll tell you the whole story," said Eddie. "Later! First, food."

He was surprised at how scary it felt to step into the open again. He had to force himself. Quick as a flick, across the desk. Down to the floor in a flash. Under the desk to wait.

It didn't take long.

BRINNNNNGGGGG! went the bell.

Chairs shifted, scraping the floor, as young Squishers rose to their feet. In a chattering rush, they surged out of the room.

Eddie listened. Hearing nothing more, he set off. Soon he was at the couch, searching the floor in wide sweeping arcs. A bit of torn paper. A hair elastic.

Suddenly the floor shook!

He darted beneath the couch just as a Squisher plopped heavily onto its cushions.

"Aaahhh," said a voice above him.

Eddie *knew* that voice. The Librarian!

Yes, there were her legs. Firm and roundish, in yellow stockings. As Eddie watched, she kicked off her shoes—dark blue, with silver buckles—and stretched out.

"Aaahhh," she said again, rubbing her feet together. "That's gooooood."

Eddie smiled. He understood completely. He often rubbed his feet together when he wanted to relax.

Paper crinkled. A moment later, a sweet smell drifted down—Eddie couldn't tell what it was, but he knew it was food. He listened again and heard one of his favorite sounds. A turning page.

She's reading, thought Eddie.

A giggle erupted up on the couch. Then a long, gleeful laugh.

A *funny* book! Eddie loved funny books. If only he could read it with her.

The Librarian had a hearty laugh. Eddie was soon chuckling along.

A few minutes later, he heard the Librarian

stir. There was a brushing sound, then something rained onto the floor. He crept closer to see.

Crumbs, he thought. Lucky me! She's a sloppy eater.

He snuck out into the open, keeping a close watch on the Librarian's feet. Only her toes moved, wiggling madly.

Raspberry muffin, thought Eddie when he reached the crumbs. Yes!

He picked up a large, moist crumb with a bit of berry, and then—unable to resist—a second smaller crumb. Leaving the Librarian still giggling, he headed back to Min.

It was slow going. The crumbs weren't heavy, but they were awkward, especially when he reached the desk. Eddie had to haul them up one at a time, using a special three-leg hold. He took the smaller crumb first, dropping it carefully at the top. He was halfway up with the larger one when . . .

BRRRIINNNGGGG!

In his shock, Eddie lost his grip.

THUD, THUD, THUD! Footsteps!

The crumb slipped. Eddie reached, grabbed—it broke into bits and tumbled to the floor.

All he could do was keep climbing. He clung for a moment at the top, jaws clenched. Then he heaved himself over. As he lay there, gathering his strength, he heard Min's voice from the tray.

"Eddie! Watch out!"

Too late, he saw the shadow on the surface of the desk.

A Squisher!

Hide! But where?

He spotted a square of yellow paper and dashed underneath it. Peeking from under his flimsy shelter, he saw Min. *She was trying to climb out of the tray.*

What was she *doing*?

Suddenly he knew. She was using herself as a decoy. She was offering up her own frail body to the Squishers.

"Nooooooo!" he whispered. "Stay there, Aunt Min. I'm fine."

She froze. Half in. Half out.

"Hey, Nathan!" said a voice. "Did you see that?"

"What?"

"Something moved. A bug or something."

"Where?"

Beneath the paper, Eddie tried to stop quivering.

"I don't see anything," said Nathan. "Anyhow, there are no bugs in the library."

At that moment, like a miracle—it was almost as if she was on the bugs' side—the Librarian spoke. "Everyone to the carpet now, please!"

Eddie collapsed onto his abdomen in relief.

And that's when he discovered a new problem. The yellow paper had a sticky edge. It was glued to his back!

"Oh, for Pete's sake," he muttered as he stumbled to the tray, wearing the yellow sticky like a roof. "Aunt Min, can you get this off me?"

Min laughed. "Don't worry. Just a jiff!" She pulled the paper one way, Eddie pulled his body the other way, and—*brrrrripp!*—the sticky tore loose.

Quickly, Eddie ran back to fetch the crumb that had survived. It was a bit squashed but still looked tasty.

Min's eyes bugged out when she saw it. "Raspberry. My favorite! Oh, Eddie, I'm in heaven."

"I had a bigger crumb, Aunt Min. I dropped it."

"This one is perfect." She gulped a piece down.

And in fact, there was plenty for them both. Aunt Min let out little chirps of satisfaction as she ate.

"I feel like a whole new bug," she said when she'd finished. Then she settled herself down, faced Eddie squarely, and folded her front legs.

"Okay," she said. "I'm listening. How did you get here, Eddie? I can't believe your parents let you go. Tell me *everything*!"

So Eddie recounted the story of his journey. He left out only two bits. That his parents had *not* given him permission to go. And that his mother had been angry at Aunt Min.

Min wasn't fooled. "Your mother's mad at me, isn't she?"

Eddie didn't answer. He had learned the hard way that it was best to stay out of his mother's quarrels with Aunt Min.

"Oh, I don't blame her," said Min. "It's *my* fault that her baby boy is stuck in a paper tray, surrounded by danger. But honestly, dear, what could I do? Some bugs are meant to be stay-at-home stick-in-the-muds, while others are destined for adventure. I can't stop myself from searching any more than your mother can stop herself from sitting like a banana slug in that crack-in-the-wall all day. We are who we are."

Eddie wondered what kind of bug *he* was. It

was a big question, he realized, and one that had caused him confusion ever since he had left home. It made him nervous right this minute, as he thought about his mother.

"It's your turn, Aunt Min," he said, changing the subject. "Tell me how you got trapped here."

Min sighed. "I wish I had a happier story to tell. . . ."

CHAPTER
6

Eddie leaned forward eagerly. After all those scary days waiting for Aunt Min to come home to the crack-in-the-wall, finally he would find out what had happened.

"Things were great at first," said Min, adjusting her legs. "When I got to the Library last Tuesday, it was as glorious as ever. The Librarian read one of my favorite books at story time—*Cloudy With a Chance of Meatballs*. It's all about food, Eddie, and I must tell you that later, when I was perishing for a bite to eat, I thought of nothing but that book. I dreamed every single day that food would fall from the sky, just as it did in the story. I imagined it falling through the skylight."

She gazed toward the skylight, remembering.

"Aunt Min?" said Eddie.

"Yes? Oh. Sorry, Eddie. Yes, last Tuesday. Well, I certainly wasn't hungry *then*. On the contrary, we had a delicious lunch together, the Librarian and I. Egg salad sandwiches. Everything was fine till late afternoon."

"And then what?"

"Hah!" said Min. "Disaster! And no one's fault but my own. I'd been wondering about those new things, Eddie—those books with no paper that some of the Squishers read."

"Tablets? iPads?" Eddie had seen them back in Room 19. He'd been curious himself.

"Exactly!" said Min. "The Librarian was reading a tablet at her desk. Then a teacher came in, looking for help—teachers wander around here all the time, Eddie, you have to watch out for them! Anyway, the Librarian went off and *left* that tablet—just sitting there on her desk. I admit, I got rather excited. A chance to satisfy my curiosity once and for all."

"Wow!" said Eddie.

"Don't cheer *yet*," said Min. "I scurried on over. And at first, it was an adventure. Hoisting myself up, getting my bearings. I felt quite proud of myself."

"Yay!" said Eddie.

Aunt Min shook her head. "Oh, Eddie! It wasn't at all what I expected. A *skating rink*, that's what it was. A glass surface. Have you ever tried to walk on glass? And as if that wasn't bad enough, it was lit up, too. Shockingly bright. Got my head in a tizz. But in spite of all that, I did it. I crawled across that thing, slipping and sliding, and I actually *read* most of the words."

"Good for you, Aunt Min."

"But when I got to the end—" Aunt Min paused, her eyes bulging.

"What?"

"Catastrophe!" said Min. "There's something on those things that makes the pages turn. Like magic, but not the good kind. All of a sudden, the pages started *changing* under me. I started on

103. But every time I moved—even a twitch—it changed! From 104 to 105, 106, 107 . . . I couldn't stop it! By 139, I was in a panic, scrambling so hard to get off that I fell. Hard! When I tried to stand up, I fell again. And again! *You* try running on glass, you'll see. Finally I fell right off the tablet. My legs were so banged up, I could barely crawl. I thought I was a goner."

Eddie tried to picture his aunt—legs broken, head muddled, staggering around.

"Somehow I dragged myself to this tray. Just in the nick of time, too. The Librarian came back."

"And you've been trapped here ever since?"

"Yes," said Min, "hiding. The Librarian is kind, of course, and I'm sure she wouldn't have squished me. But she might very well have thrown me out the window, all with the best of intentions. I saw her do that to a ladybug once."

"Oh, no! We would never have seen you again."

Min nodded. "We have to be so careful. I'll tell you one thing, Eddie, I will *never* step on one of those things again. Nothing but paper books for Min from now on."

Eddie, who had been secretly longing to try a tablet himself, nodded. "Me, too."

Min cocked her head. "Oh, I don't know. Maybe you could figure it out."

"It would never be the same," said Eddie.

It was true. Half the fun of reading was the paper. The spongy softness beneath his feet. The springiness as he moved from word to word.

A burst of laughter interrupted his thoughts. Young Squishers—children!—on the story-time carpet.

"Hey," said Eddie. "They're reading a funny book."

"Good," said Min. "I could use a laugh."

They crept to the front of the paper tray, where they could get a good view. The Librarian was sitting in the story-time chair, facing a class of giggling children and holding up a book showing goofy-looking black-and-white cows.

"First grade," murmured Aunt Min.

"What's the book?" asked Eddie.

"Click, Clack, Moo: Cows That Type."

"What?" said Eddie. "Hey, wait! Cows can't type."

Min gave him a playful shove. "How do you know? Maybe there's a farm somewhere full of cows who *can* type. Shh. Listen."

So they did. The cows in the story were wacky enough to make even an achy old bug like Min laugh. By the end, she and Eddie were giggling along with the children.

They returned to their hiding spot reluctantly.

"Well, that did me good," said Min. "Just like medicine."

Eddie nodded. He swayed as if in a strong breeze.

"Oh, Eddie! You're falling over." Min's huge eyes swiveled to inspect him. "Well, of course, you are. You must be exhausted after everything you've done today. What a terrible auntie I am, keeping you awake all this time."

Eddie didn't argue. Being mostly nocturnal, he

had a hard time staying awake in daylight even on a normal day. His abdomen drooped.

"There now," said Min. "It's way past your nap time. Why don't you have a nice little snooze?"

So that's what Eddie did. He found an empty bit of tray and settled down to rest.

"Eddie?" said Min as he drifted off.

"Mmm?"

"Thank you, dear. Thank you for coming."

CHAPTER
7

Eddie slept like a rock.

Or maybe he slept more like a shiny green pebble. Because if you could have peeked at him as he lay there on the bottom of the tray, that's what he would have looked like to you. A small, smooth, still green pebble. Until . . .

BRRRIIIINNNGGGG!

At the sound of the bell, Eddie rose to his feet. He glanced around, then trotted to the front of the tray.

"Hey, Aunt Min. Which bell was that?"

"End of day. See? The children are leaving."

Together they watched as the young Squishers wandered off to wherever they spent the night.

"Teatime now," said Min. "The Librarian likes to linger for a cup after school."

And sure enough, the next sound was water boiling in a kettle at the far end of the Library.

"She has a small office back there," said Min.

When the Librarian brought her tea to the desk, Eddie was excited to get an up-close view.

"Gosh!" he said. "Isn't she something!"

He stretched to get a good look. The Librarian was a roundish kind of Squisher with a cheerful face and a plump body. Everything about her was colorful. Red hair, purple glasses, turquoise top.

"She's like a butterfly!" said Eddie in astonishment.

"Hsst, Eddie, get down."

But Min needn't have worried. The Librarian was busy opening a book. A moment later, she chuckled.

"It's the same book she was reading at lunchtime," whispered Eddie. "She was laughing then, too. Do you think she'll leave it behind?"

"Shh," said Min.

Together, they listened to sipping and clinking, and pages turning, and now and then laughing. Finally, there was humming as the Librarian stood up.

"Darn!" said Eddie as she popped the book into her purse.

She put on her coat. It was as red as a ripe apple, and her wool hat was as blue as the evening sky.

Eddie looked more closely.

"Gosh," he said, watching her as she left the Library. "The Librarian is *very* round, isn't she?"

Min nodded. "Didn't you know? She's going to have a baby."

"A baby? Just one?"

Another nod from Min. "They only have one baby at a time, those Squishers. Silly, isn't it? Hardly worth the trouble. But the bad part is—she's going to leave the Library."

"Leave?" Eddie twitched uncomfortably. "Why?"

"To look after the baby. It's ridiculous, I know. Babies should be able to look after *themselves* after the first few weeks. And for goodness sake, there'll only be *one*."

She sighed and continued. "Squisher babies are different. Helpless. Pathetic. Our Librarian will be gone for some time."

"Oh, no!" Eddie had only known the Librarian briefly, but he already felt very fond of her.

A new thought struck him. "Who's going to look after the Library?"

Min sighed. "Don't ask, Eddie. I wish . . ."
She stopped.

"What do you wish? What's wrong?"

"Nothing," said Min. "At least, nothing yet. I'm just . . . a little nervous, that's all. About what's going to happen when the Librarian leaves. But don't *you* worry. By that time, you'll be home with your family."

"We both will," said Eddie. "Listen, Aunt Min, I've been thinking. Why don't we leave tonight? Go home."

"We?" said Min.

Eddie stared back, puzzled. "Of course. You and me."

"But Eddie—"

"I don't *want* to go," said Eddie. "But we have to."

It was true. In the short time since he'd arrived, he'd been totally enchanted by the Library. But Min's safety was more important. "We're living on top of a *desk*, Aunt Min! The most dangerous place in the school. We have to leave."

"Eddie," said Min slowly, "look at me. Really look. Can't you see? I'm on my last legs." She wiggled the four that still worked. Even those movements were feeble.

"Don't say that, Aunt Min. I can *help*. You can lean on me."

She shook her head. "Think about it. If we were down on the floor, we might stagger along somehow. But how would I get to the floor?"

"I'll carry you down."

Min shook her head again. "That's sweet. But remember how hard it was to get a crumb up here? Do you really think you could carry a whole bug down?"

He didn't answer. He hated that she was right. He was too small. He didn't have enough strength. And a horrible thought crossed his mind. What if he dropped her?

"But you *can't* stay here!" he cried. "You know you can't!"

"Sometimes we don't get a choice," she said. "My injuries will take time to heal. And that's fine, I can wait—I'm a tough old bug. But you? *You* must go back. Your parents will be frantic."

"Aunt Min—"

"Go. I'll be fine."

Eddie gulped. He had never heard such a big, brave lie in his life. Dreamy, he might be, even foolish. But he wasn't stupid. And Eddie knew, as surely as he knew his own name, what would happen to Min if he left her there—trapped, injured, and unable to get food.

"No," he said in the firmest voice he could muster. "If you're staying, so am I."

What followed next was an excruciatingly long argument. It would take several pages, in fact, to tell you the details of how Min coaxed and threatened and reminded Eddie over and over about his worried parents, about the example he should set for his brothers and sisters, and about the various risks of staying, which were somehow just fine for *her* but much too dangerous for *him*. All you really need to know is this: Eddie waited patiently till his aunt was finished and then said in a surprisingly certain voice, "You're wasting your breath."

Min stomped her front foot. "Oh, Eddie! When did you get so stubborn?"

"Runs in the family."

She tried not to smile.

"Okay," she said finally, "I can't force you. But this makes me responsible. If something were to happen to you—well, honestly, Eddie, your mother would have me for breakfast! Promise me you'll be *extremely* careful, especially when the Squishers are around."

"I promise."

"No daydreaming? You'll pay attention?" She gave him a sharp look.

"I promise."

"Good. Now it's my turn for a nap. All this excitement since you arrived—I can't believe I've stayed awake all day."

"Go rest," said Eddie. "I'll stand guard while you sleep."

Min obeyed, making herself a bed atop a crumpled tissue. "Don't wander off now."

"I won't."

Seconds later, she was snoring. Stepping carefully so as not to rattle any papers, Eddie crept out of the tray.

He stood guard, just as he'd promised. But after a long period of watchfulness, during which not one single thing happened except for increasingly loud snores from his aunt, he realized—there was nothing to guard against. The Squishers had all gone home.

"Hmph," he said out loud.

He was bored.

But how could he be bored? This was the *Library*!

He wasn't *seeing* the Library, that was why. And what was the point of being in the Library if he didn't experience it?

A tingle ran through his feet, tiny but quite thrilling. Eddie laughed, remembering how nervous his feet had been on the journey to the Library. Now, suddenly, they were brave and wanted to explore.

But . . . no. He had promised Aunt Min he'd stay close.

His feet argued back. The *desk* was close, they said. Up till now, Eddie had stayed near the paper tray. But the desk was much larger than that. Eddie could look across it and see the fantastic jumble of things he had noticed when he first arrived—things the Librarian must need in her job.

What could they be?

As he started to walk, his feet tingled harder.

They seemed to have minds of their own.

Pencils he found in abundance. Also, pens. A Librarian must have to write many things, thought Eddie. Sure enough, he found some. A list with the heading, "Kindergarten Story Time" followed by the titles of three books. Another list said, "Research—Solar System."

Eddie's feet carried him on, past a glass bowl filled with gold stars. Behind these rose a giant tape dispenser and a huge box of tissues. Tucked between, like a joke, was a plastic duck. It swung when Eddie pushed it. (He had to run to get out of the way!)

Looming above everything was a computer, its screen an enormous blank eye. In the daytime, it must have been filled with bright images. Now it was empty and gray. Smaller gray things—a mystery to Eddie—were attached to the big computer. Must be a computer family, thought Eddie.

A framed photo caught his eye. He scuttled over. The picture showed a man and a woman hugging a curly haired dog. Eddie recognized the woman immediately. The Librarian!

Beside the photo was a blue stamp pad, left open. Eddie knew all about stamp pads. The Teacher had one in Room 19. Pa had stumbled onto it one dark night and had come home *blue*. He'd left footprints all over the Teacher's desk.

Eddie kept his distance from the stamp pad.

He found more yellow stickies. They were everywhere! The Librarian must really *like* stickies.

He also found a mysterious straw basket, woven in lots of different colors. It was wider at the top than at the bottom, which made it extremely difficult to climb.

What was inside? Eddie couldn't stand not knowing. Slowly, with great effort, he hauled himself all the way to the top.

It was worth the climb. At first the odd collection of objects in the basket made no sense. But then Eddie recognized one—a toy train with a smiling face.

"Thomas the Tank Engine!" he cried.

Recognizing Thomas made Eddie suspect that the other objects might also be clues to books. He made a list in his head so he could ask Aunt Min about them later:

- a purple plastic purse
- a box of crayons
- a toy pig with big ears, wearing a red dress
- a little silver jingle bell
- a pair of children's glasses with round lenses
- a tall hat with red-and-white stripes
- a long feathery pink thing that looked like clothing

When Eddie saw the feathery thing—so soft to sleep on—he thought of Aunt Min. He tried to take it back for her. But it was too hard to drag.

Fortunately, climbing *out* of the basket was not hard at all. When Eddie reached the top rim, he just dropped down.

His last stop, closest to the Librarian's chair, was the best stop of all. The Librarian's teacup! The one she had been drinking from earlier. Eddie crept closer, admiring the lavish pink roses. When he reached the saucer, he glanced down and . . .

Yes!

There was *tea* spilled in the saucer. Lovely, clear, amber tea. Gone cold now—he tested it with his antennae. But still delicious, as he discovered when he took a sip.

Aunt Min would be so pleased.

Bursting with his news, he ran back to tell her. But she was still in a deep snooze.

"Hmph," muttered Eddie.

He settled down to wait. He watched the clouds drift in snowy puffs across the skylight. He stared out at the trees, their leaves shimmering in the late afternoon sun. He thought about his parents—and then stopped because he was almost positive they were angry with him.

However angry they might be, he knew what he had to do. Look after Aunt Min.

He checked on her again.

"Hmph!" he repeated.

He wiggled. He stretched. He stared at his feet. Tingling again . . .

And that's when Eddie (or possibly his feet) figured something out.

At that moment, the Library was *his*. All his. Not just the paper tray. Not just the desk. The whole magnificent, glorious, magical room. For however long it lasted, this Library—and every book in it—belonged to a bug named Eddie.

He might never have this chance again. . . .

CHAPTER 8

Giddy with excitement, Eddie shinnied down the desk.

He knew exactly where he was going. Away he ran, making a beeline for the fancy red cabinet at the back of the Library, his feet tingling so hard, they were practically on fire.

As he passed the story-time carpet, something caught his eye. Something lying on top. Could it be . . .

If Eddie had stopped to think, he might have remembered his father's warning. Watch out for carpets! But he didn't think. What Eddie did instead—in a great *unthinking* rush—was turn, scramble onto the carpet, and run toward the book that lay open in the middle.

After only three steps, he stopped. He barked out a laugh. This was the most peculiar "running" he had ever done. Definitely the slowest. His legs kept dropping between tufts of wool. His body rose or sank with every move he made.

His father was right. Carpets were weird.

But he struggled on gamely till at last he reached the book. He climbed onto the left-hand page and looked around.

A chapter book. He had never read one of these alone before, only with Aunt Min's help. The page was old and had obviously been read many times. He could tell by the way it felt beneath his feet. Worn. Soft. Fuzzy.

The page was so comfortable, in fact, that Eddie did something he'd never done before.

He lay down on the book.

"Like a feather bed," thought Eddie. He had never actually *felt* a feather bed, but he'd heard about one in a princess story.

He did a little roll, breathing in the book's smells. Dog. Old grass. Happiness.

Rolling again, he picked up a new smell. Tuna fish. Someone had read this book while eating a *tuna* sandwich. Yes, there! He could see the oily stain on the paper.

What an excellent book, thought Eddie. Good for sleeping. Good for rolling. Good for smelling. And most of all, good for . . .

He headed to the top-left corner. Then, walking across the letters one after another, he began to read.

. . . the Littles were up early as a general rule. Stuart was a great help to his parents and to his older brother George, because of his small size and because he could do things that a mouse can do and was agreeable about doing them.

Eddie's mandibles went slack in astonishment. Of all the books in the Library, the one that was waiting on the story-time carpet was about . . . a mouse! A mouse was bigger than a bug, he knew that. But not a *lot* bigger. And a mouse certainly knew how it felt to be tiny in a big world.

Eddie was entranced.

Letter by letter, word by word, he read on. Stuart's mother (not a mouse, for some reason) had lost her ring down the drain of a sink. How could she get it back? Stuart was the only one small enough—Eddie *loved* this part—to crawl into the drain to fetch it. Stuart was also clever about holding onto a piece of string, so that he could be pulled out. In fact, there was a drawing in the book of Stuart being lifted out of the drain, his mother's ring safely around his neck.

But at the bottom of the page—

The words stopped! Right in the middle of the story.

Eddie snorted with annoyance. He hated when this happened. What came next? Was Stuart's mother excited to get her ring back? Was she proud of her son?

If only he could turn the page.

Never had he done such a thing on his own. The few times he had helped Aunt Min to turn pages, he'd discovered that it wasn't easy. And some pages, he knew, were too heavy for *any* bug to turn. (Except for Grandpa, of course. Grandpa George had been so big and strong, he could turn any page he liked.)

Eddie stared at the page. It didn't *look* heavy.

He headed for the book's outer edge, as Aunt Min had taught him to do, and carefully crawled underneath the page. He continued to crawl until he reached the middle of the book, where the page above him was sewn in. Then, pushing his head really *hard* against that page, he kept crawling. Push, push, push, push, push. This was the difficult part—like pushing an avalanche *up* a mountainside. He wasn't actually moving much, but yes . . . the page was rising! Push, push, push, push, push. Higher now. And higher. One final mighty *heeeaaave!*

The page, with a great *FLAP* of air, flopped over.

And so did Eddie. He did a somersault!

Laughing, he got to his feet. Then he looked around. He was standing on two *new* pages. He had done it! All by himself. He wished Aunt Min was here to see.

He scampered to the top of the page and read the next sentence.

"Oh, my brave little son," said Mrs. Little proudly, as she kissed Stuart and thanked him.

Feeling a rush of pleasure on Stuart's behalf,

Eddie read on. And on. And on. He forgot about Aunt Min. He forgot about the Library. He even forgot about the school. He was deep inside the story now, lost in Stuart's world. . . .

KA-BANG! The Library door crashed open.

Eddie jumped.

Rrrrrumble, rrrrrumble.

"Uh-oh." He knew that sound.

The Cleaner!

Yes! There he was, pushing his big cart full of supplies. Pail, mop, dusters, and . . .

Vacuum cleaner!

How could Eddie have forgotten? Every evening, the Cleaner came to Ferny Creek Elementary. Every evening, the bugs made sure they were safely home before he arrived. It was the number one rule in Eddie's family. *How could he forget?*

Rrrrumble, rrrrumble. The cart rolled across the Library on rubber wheels, heading straight for . . .

Eddie.

CHAPTER 9

Eddie jumped like a flea. In two stupendous leaps, he reached the bottom of *Stuart Little* and threw himself onto—

"Oh, no!" he remembered. "The carpet!"

It was as if it had been *waiting* for him. The second he landed, it seized his legs.

"Oh, please," begged Eddie. "Not now!"

He thrashed with all his strength against the tufts. He forced his body forward. But every time he freed his legs, the carpet grabbed them again. It was like walking in quicksand. And with each step, he listened for it. The terrible *ROARRRR* that could only mean—

The vacuum cleaner!

The vacuum cleaner, as Eddie knew only too well, was the most horrifying machine in the world. Every evening, it rolled across the floor, sucking up everything in its path. Coins, dirt, paper clips, crumbs. Even—and most terribly— insects. Living or dead, the vacuum didn't care. It sucked entire families into its belly of filth. One dreadful evening, Min had seen the Cleaner empty the vacuum's belly. She would never speak about it again. She said the carnage was too awful to describe.

And now that very same vacuum was right behind Eddie—just waiting to do its foul work. Would Eddie take his last breath in a bag of dirt?

He struggled on through the carpet. He flailed and thrashed. At long last, he dropped, exhausted, onto the pale linoleum floor.

As he lay there gasping, he listened again. Where was it? The *ROARRRR*?

He looked around.

The Cleaner stood quietly beside his cart, his back to Eddie. Behind him waited the vacuum, its cord still wound up.

Eddie did a little leap of joy. The vacuum had *not* gobbled him up! It hadn't even been turned on. Astounded by his luck, he headed for the desk.

When he heard a strange sound behind him, he picked up his pace but felt no real panic. It was only a bit of splashing.

"Splashing?" thought Eddie.

He turned to face—

A gargantuan tangle of ugly gray snakes! Coming straight at him!

No, he thought. Not snakes.

The mop!

Its huge tangled ropes—filthy and foul—were pushing a wave of water. The wave hit! It lifted poor Eddie right off his feet. And before he could catch his breath, the monster mop had swallowed him whole. Deep into its innards went Eddie, tossed like a grain of sand—forward, backward, sideways. If he could have fought back, he would have. But the mop was too strong. A tsunami! Its thick, murky water was suffocating.

All Eddie could do was curl up.

Wait.

Forward, backward, sideways.

Forward, backward, sideways.

He would never know how long it lasted. At some point, the mop was hoisted up—with Eddie still inside—and dumped with a mighty *SPLASH* into deep water.

The force of it released him.

Suddenly, with a great *SCHWOOOP*, the mop was gone. Eddie swirled helplessly in its wake as he rose to the surface.

Bobbing up, he stared bleary-eyed at his surroundings. He was floating in a metal pail. Coating the water's surface was a layer of scum. Here and there floated yellow-gray suds.

"Help!" yelled Eddie as a broken potato chip floated past.

But there was no help.

He scrabbled frantically with his legs. A new fear arose. "Am I going to drown?"

Then he remembered. "Water bugs!"

Aunt Min had read a nonfiction book about them—where they lived, what they ate, how they swam.

"How *did* they swim?" Eddie searched his memory. Something about paddling their legs. Like oars.

Had Eddie ever seen an oar? Never.

"Try!" he said out loud. "Try!" And with only the tiniest notion of what paddling might be, Eddie paddled. Mostly this turned out to be moving all his legs at once as fast as they could go. Somehow it kept him from sinking.

But for how long?

His paddling took him to the inner wall of the pail. It was shiny and rose high and smooth. Impossible to climb. As Eddie grasped in vain for a foothold, his heart sank.

He could *never* crawl out of this pail. Not in a billion years.

"Think!" he told himself. "Think about this pail."

He searched his memory again. Once he had

peeked from the crack-in-the-wall as the Cleaner pushed his mop around the room. The Cleaner would return to the pail every now and then and put the mop in the water.

Yes! Eddie was now almost sure that the mop was going to plunge into this pail *again*. He knew what he had to do. He just hoped he could stay afloat long enough to do it.

The waiting seemed to take forever. At last he heard the Cleaner's footsteps returning. *THUD. THUD. THUD.*

Eddie paddled to the middle of the pail. He screwed up his courage. This was going to be difficult. Maybe impossible. And it was going to hurt!

"Be brave," he told himself. "Like Stuart Little."

He waited while the Cleaner picked up the mop. *SHLUP!*

He waited while the Cleaner wrung the mop out in a special little side compartment of the pail. *SHWOOSH!*

He waited, reminding himself that sometimes the way you get *out* of trouble is the same way you got *in*.

Then suddenly—*yes, now!*—the mop dropped fast, into the pail. Eddie stopped paddling. As the mop hit, he reached with all six legs and grabbed on. He fastened his body like a burr to one of the soggy ropes, and as the mop rose up, he held on. Water poured in a powerful cascade over Eddie's body, trying to dislodge him, trying to force him back into the pail. But he held tight.

He felt a wild *swing* as the mop dipped again into the little compartment for a wringing out. But he knew *that* was coming too. He clung fiercely as the ropes were squeezed hard against the metal. *SHWOOSH!*

"Oof!" went Eddie! It was worse than he'd expected. The squeeze was fierce enough to crack a bug's exoskeleton. Eddie's guts felt ready to pop.

But before that could happen, the mop rose up again. Eddie hung on. Yes! Time for his final move. As the mop was lowered to the floor—he let go.

He hit the floor an instant before the mop. Immediately, he zigged to the side—just before the Cleaner's big black shoe came down. *CRASH!*

And there—like a miracle—was the desk.

Eddie ran for his life!

When he was safe behind the desk leg, he scrunched himself into a small, trembling ball. He listened as the sloshing sounds went on and on. When he heard the *ROARRRR* of the vacuum, he shuddered, grateful to be out of its path. He waited to hear the cart *rrrrumble* down the hall. Then, finally, he began the long, slow climb up the desk. Never in his life had he felt so tired.

Aunt Min was waiting, wringing her feet. "Eddie? Is that really *you*? Holy dung beetles! What on earth happened?"

Eddie tried to explain, but he didn't get far—

"I thought you were getting stomped on!" cried Min. "Or sucked up! Or drowned by that dratted mop!"

"A little of each," mumbled Eddie. "But I'm okay now."

"No, you are *not* okay. You look ghastly!"

So he told her the story as calmly as he could, trying to make it sound less terrible. Aunt Min made gasping sounds anyway. When he'd finished, she just stared at him, jaws open.

"That," she said finally, "was a *horror* story. I don't think I've ever heard a scarier one. And yet . . . here you are, Eddie. Safe. Alive!" She touched his dirty exoskeleton as if to make sure. "Do you have any idea how scared I was?"

"I know. I'm sorry. I should never have wandered off without telling you."

"You've got *that* right!" she said.

And then, surprisingly, she laughed. "Just look at you. What a draggletailed mess!"

He shrugged.

"You remind me of myself when I was younger."

"I *do*?" said Eddie.

"Unfortunately, yes," said Min, "including the kind of reckless behavior that almost got me killed. Oh, Eddie, what if you hadn't come back?"

"I know," he said. And of course, he did know because he remembered how scared *he* had felt, waiting for Min to return home. "I just . . . I just really wanted to see the Library."

Min stared into his eyes for a moment. Then she nodded.

"I'll be more careful from now on," he said.

"You darned well better!" said Min. "Now let me say one last thing. And that is—you surprise me, Eddie. No. More than that. You amaze me. How you managed to survive that ordeal with so little experience of the world . . . well, I can hardly take it in."

Eddie smiled. "I kind of amazed myself," he said.

It was true. Looking back at the things he had faced on his adventure—he was already thinking of it as the Attack of the Killer Mop—it was as if it must have happened to some other bug. Someone bigger. Braver. Then he looked down at his body, streaked gray with muck, and he knew for a fact that it had been *him* in that pail.

"It helped to remember the water bugs," he told his aunt.

"Ah, yes," said Min. "That was a good book."

"Excellent," said Eddie. He had never imagined that the swimming habits of water bugs would turn out to be so spectacularly useful.

"Stuart Little, too," he added. "It helped to think about him. How he went down the drain of the sink."

"Books," murmured Aunt Min. "They light the way."

Eddie nodded. He glanced again at his filthy exoskeleton. "Come with me, Aunt Min. I want to show you something."

He led her to the teacup. "See?" He pointed at the cold tea in the saucer.

"Perfect. You need a bath."

Eddie shook his head. "Let's save it for drinking. I'll just use a bit to wash up."

Fortunately, there was a tissue nearby, drooping out of the huge tissue box. Eddie ripped off a shred and dipped it into the tea. Then he handed it to his aunt. She wiped his shell all over till he was back to his shiny self.

"What color!" said Min. "How did that Cleaner miss seeing you? Needs new glasses. But me? I love your shade of green, Eddie. It reminds me of the Big Woods."

"Do you miss the Big Woods, Aunt Min?"

"Oh, yes," she said softly. "But I look at it this way. If we'd stayed in the Big Woods, I would never have learned to read. And *that* . . . well . . . I can't even imagine."

They drank their fill of tea, then strolled back to their home in the tray. Aunt Min rocked and lurched as she walked, and Eddie tried to support her. But at some point, he realized that *she* was supporting *him*.

Aunt Min noticed, too. "Are you all right, Eddie?"

"Dizzy," he said.

"Of course you are. After all you've been through. You'll feel better tomorrow, you'll see.

Everything will be better in the morning."

Eddie nodded and sank gratefully onto the tray.

But when the sun rose the next day, things were *not* better.

Everything, in fact, was terribly, horribly worse.

CHAPTER
10

There was a clock in the Ferny Creek School Library. It hung high on the wall above the computer desks. It had a big hand and a little hand that went around and around and around.

Eddie and Min never gave it a glance. They didn't understand it, and they didn't need to. Like all bugs, they had an inner sense of time that didn't depend on the kind of clocks, watches, and calendars that you and I must rely on. So when the Librarian didn't turn up at her usual time the next morning, they noticed.

"She should be here by now," said Min. "She always arrives early."

They waited.

The Library waited, too. The shadows of daybreak had lifted, allowing the new books to sparkle in the morning light. The posters, feeling the sun, came cheerily to life. "READ!" they said. Even the hush in the air felt heavy— as if filled with stories waiting to be read.

Suddenly the big school door clanged! The hallway filled with voices. First the low voices of adult Squishers. Then the higher, louder voices of children. *THUD, THUD, THUD* went the feet. Listening, Eddie couldn't help remembering how, only a few days before, he had been trapped—tiny and terrorized—in the great crush of school opening. He hoped he would never have to endure *that* again.

BRRRRINGGG! went the bell to start school.

The Library stayed quiet.

"What could be keeping her?" asked Min. "I hope she's not sick."

They didn't find out till Announcements.

The bugs usually ignored Announcements.

The Announcements, broadcast each morning through the school, were about sports teams and birthdays and report cards. Nothing of concern to a bug.

But today Eddie and Min listened.

"We are pleased to announce," said the Announcements, "that Ms. Laurel from the Library had her baby last night. In fact, she had *three* babies! Triplet baby girls. We were expecting this news, of course, but not quite so soon. At any rate, we are happy to congratulate Ms. Laurel and her husband on these exciting new additions to their family."

Min stiffened, her whole body suddenly alert.

"Ms. Laurel," the Announcements continued, "has now gone on leave. She will be replaced in the Library by Ms. Grisch. We know you will all give Ms. Grisch a wonderful Ferny Creek welcome."

"Aunt Min?" said Eddie. "Are you all right?'"

At the word *Grisch*, she had made a choking sound.

When she didn't answer, he tried again. "Who's Ms. Grisch? Do you know her?"

"No." Min spoke slowly. "But I know that . . . name. I've heard it at meetings, here in the Library. Oh, dear. I was afraid of this."

"Why?" asked Eddie, alarmed now. "What's wrong? She's a librarian, isn't she?"

Min shook her head. "I don't believe she is, or ever was. Her brother is the new superintendent of schools. From what I understand, he can hire who he wants."

"Is *his* name Grisch, too?"

She nodded.

"Rhymes with *squish*," said Eddie. "I don't like them already."

"Their *name*," said Min quietly, "is the least of our problems."

"Oh," said Eddie. He was nervous about his next question, but he asked it anyway. "What's the *worst* of our problems?"

"I'm not sure yet. But this is definitely not good news. Mr. Grisch doesn't like libraries. He thinks they're a waste of money."

"Aunt Min?"

"Yes?

"What's money?"

"Oh, Eddie, you don't know?"

"Not really."

"Well, why would you?" said Min. "Money, my dear, is a foolish thing the Squishers have invented to make their lives more difficult. Do *not* try to understand it, it's impossible. All you need to know is this—libraries need money to exist. And this new superintendent, who's in charge of the money, does not like to give it to libraries."

"Aunt Min?" said Eddie.

"Yes?"

"I don't get it. Is the Library in trouble?"

"It might be. We'll have to wait and see." She let out a sigh. "Try not to worry, Eddie."

At that, the bugs went quiet. In the background, the Announcements told about Wacky Hat Friday and a lunchtime basketball game.

Eddie had another thought. A more hopeful one. "Maybe our Librarian will come back!" he said. "Maybe she'll leave her grubs at home and come back here really soon."

Min shook her head. "Didn't you hear? She had three babies. That's rare for Squishers. And it makes things worse."

"Why?" Eddie's mother always said—the more, the merrier.

"It means," said Min, "that she will fuss over them for a long time. Squisher babies, as I've told you, are helpless. They just *lie* there. Three will be more work than one."

"So she's not coming back?"

Min shook her head. "Not for ages."

"Oh," said Eddie.

There was a long silence as he tried to take this in.

"Aunt Min?"

"Yes?"

"I wish *you* could be the new Librarian."

Min smiled. "What a sweet thing to say. I have often had that wish myself. I would *love* to be a librarian. If only I were taller."

For a moment both bugs allowed themselves to imagine. . . .

"Aunt Min?" said Eddie. "Is there anything we can do?"

She took a deep breath. "Let's cross our fingers for luck. Oh, wait, we don't *have* fingers. Let's cross our antennae instead."

Eddie laughed. Both bugs crossed their antennae.

"And don't worry!" said Aunt Min.

Well, of course, there's nothing like being told not to worry to get you into the worst worry knot of your entire life. For the next few minutes, Eddie worried intensely. He worried about Min's injuries. He worried about the vanished Librarian and her helpless grubs. And he worried about the strange, foolish, mysterious thing called money.

And then he did a very sensible thing—

He fell asleep.

CHAPTER 11

Eddie awoke to the sound of Squishers talking. One was the Principal, whose voice was familiar from visits to Room 19. The other voice was odd and husky, somewhere between a purr and a growl.

Rubbing his face, Eddie joined Aunt Min at their lookout spot in the tray. "Is that her? Ms. Grisch?"

Min nodded.

The Squishers were standing on the story-time carpet. Ms. Grisch faced the desk, allowing Eddie and Min to see her clearly.

She was tall and thin and wore tiny metal-rimmed glasses that reflected the light. She was also surprisingly colorless. Her skin, her hair, even her clothing had a washed-out quality.

"What a large room," she said softly. "And so much glass." She pointed at the skylight, then gestured at the expanse of windows.

"Oh, yes," said the Principal proudly. "We're lucky to have such a library. Everyone loves looking at the forest. We watch it change through the seasons. Why it's almost like being out—"

"I was thinking of the *cost*, Mr. Steadman," said Ms. Grisch.

"The—what? Cost?"

"It costs a fortune to keep a room this size heated, especially with all these windows. We have such long, cold winters, don't we? Have you thought about the cost?"

"Oh!" said the Principal, surprised. "Well, I hadn't really—"

"And yet even though it's such a large room, it's so . . . crowded." Ms. Grisch moved soundlessly toward the shelves. "All these dusty old books."

She plucked one out and blew on it. "Who takes

care of the dust, Mr. Steadman? Plenty of people are allergic to dust. Me, for instance. I certainly can't be expected to do any dusting."

She held the book out for him to see.

"No, no, of course not." Mr. Steadman sounded a little rattled. "We have an excellent maintenance crew. Mr. Iversen cleans every evening. I will ask him to be more thorough with the dusting."

Taking the book from her, he put it back on the shelf where it belonged. "And actually, Ms. Grisch, they aren't all *old* books. Not at all! Ms. Laurel went to great trouble to find the best new books that—"

"Oh, you don't have to tell me about Ms. Laurel." Ms. Grisch waved a long, thin hand. "I know all about Ms. Laurel and her fondness for new books."

"You do?"

"Oh, yes. Have you had a close look at these books, Mr. Steadman? Many of them . . . well, I don't mean to criticize, but the word *rubbish* comes to mind."

"Rubbish?" The Principal sounded astonished.

"See for yourself." She pointed at the shelves. "I can already tell you. Series books, storybooks, books with nothing but pictures. Books that are actually called *nonsense* verse! Violent, frightening books filled with vampires and wizards. Comic books. Joke books. Magic books. Even *love* stories! Need I go on?"

"Oh, dear," said the Principal.

"Not to mention the money that's gone into those tablets. If the children want to use *tablets*, Mr. Steadman, surely their parents can purchase them at home. If, that is, they're so foolish as to entrust expensive electronic equipment to a child."

"Well, I—"

"We can do better here, I'm sure," purred Ms. Grisch. "We can have a more . . . *compact* collection of books and equipment. More appropriate. I'll be glad to weed things out."

"I see," said the Principal, who didn't seem to see at all.

He opened his mouth to say more, but just then Ms. Grisch tripped over the story-time chair. It was only a small trip, just a stumble, and she righted herself immediately. But her reaction was huge.

She *kicked* the story-time chair.

Min gasped.

"See what I mean?" said Ms. Grisch. "Overcrowded. How many children have tripped on this chair, Mr. Steadman?"

"Well, er, none that I know of, but—"

"It's a safety hazard. We can certainly clear *that* out."

"Really? But Ms. Laurel—"

"Ms. Laurel did her best, I am sure," said Ms. Grisch. "But her mind was obviously on other things. Now that she's gone, we can make some sensible changes."

"Changes?" The Principal looked around in confusion. "But surely that would cost—"

"Money? Oh, Mr. Steadman, I agree. We do *not* want to waste money. There has been far too much money wasted here already. It's everywhere you look. Here, for instance."

Striding over to the comfy couch, she kicked that, too. Not hard. But Min gasped anyway.

"A couch?" said Ms. Grisch in the same tone of voice she might have used to say, "A rat?"

Mr. Steadman stared at it in confusion. "Well . . . yes. A couch."

"Is this meant to be a *living room*, Mr. Steadman? I mean, what is the point of an over-stuffed couch in a school? And the cushions?

The stuffed animals? Are we in a *bedroom*?" She picked up a plush bear.

"Well, actually, that's Winnie-the-Pooh. He's a *puppet*," said the Principal. "Most of these . . . er . . . stuffed animals are story puppets for—"

"I know what they are," said Ms. Grisch. "I also know what they cost! Times are hard. Times are tough. These children might as well learn that, right from the start."

"Yes, but—"

"I'm sure you agree they need to learn about the value of money. They also need to learn about the value of hard work. Work, Mr. Steadman! No one has ever made money by reading a *book*."

"Well, perhaps not immediately," said the Principal. "But studies show that children who read regularly—"

"Studies, shmuddies," said Ms. Grisch. "If you just—"

Suddenly she froze. Her body went stiff.

"Stay where you are," she hissed at the Principal.

Moving extremely slowly, she sidled, crab-like, toward the graphic novel display. With a stealth that made her almost invisible, she reached for a book. Slowly, she raised it above her head.

CRASH! The book came smashing down on a small table.

"Fly," said Ms. Grisch calmly.

Turning the book over, she examined the cover with satisfaction. "At least, it *used* to be a fly."

"Oh!" cried Min. "Oh! Oh! Oh! Did you *see* that, Eddie? Did you *see* what that monster did?"

"Shh, Aunt Min. She'll hear."

But Ms. Grisch, having tossed the graphic novel back into its rack—*with the dead fly still attached*—was once again focused on Mr. Steadman. "Where were we? Oh, yes, changes."

The Principal, who had been pulling at his collar, took this opportunity to speak up. "Now, Ms. Grisch, I do see your point. It's just that . . . well, our students are really very fond of this Library. Many say it's their favorite place in the school.

Ms. Laurel felt that only the most interesting—"

"Interesting?" said Ms. Grisch. "Interesting? You're the principal, Mr. Steadman. You should be thinking about what's *good* for your students. Not what is interesting. Do you think *I* ever did anything interesting as a child?"

"Well ... er ... I couldn't say," said the Principal. "Perhaps not?"

"Never!" said Ms. Grisch. "My parents knew what was good for me. Drills, Mr. Steadman. They drilled my brother and me—yes, every day. Multiplication tables, spelling, capital cities. And look at us now."

"Oh, indeed," said the Principal. "Indeed."

"Well, then, good." Ms. Grisch clasped her hands together tightly and rocked slightly on her heels. "Excellent. We understand each other."

The Principal didn't have much hair, but what he did have was standing up oddly on his head. "I don't quite ... well, let me say ... anyway, welcome to Ferny Creek Elementary, Ms. Grisch. It's good of you to come at short notice."

"My pleasure," said Ms. Grisch. "My brother asked me weeks ago."

"He did? Oh. Well. I suppose . . . yes, of course."

The Library door went *KA-BANG* as Ms. Grisch and Mr. Steadman left the room.

It was a full minute before Eddie or Min could speak.

"Oh . . . my . . . gosh," said Eddie finally. "She's awful!"

"Worse than awful," said Min, still trembling from the death of the fly. "That was downright gruesome! She's the most grisly Squisher I have ever seen."

"A Grischer!" said Eddie.

"Exactly," said Min. "A Grischer."

But Eddie was still struggling to understand. "She wants to change everything. How can that happen? Won't the other Squishers stop her?"

"The Principal *tried* to argue. You heard him, Eddie. He was like a cricket facing a praying mantis."

"A mantis," said Eddie. "Yes, *that's* what she's like. Tall and strange and scary."

Min shuddered. "A mantis uses camouflage to hide itself. Did you notice that about her? She has no more color than a moth."

"She's stealthy, too," said Eddie. "Just like a mantis."

"We'll have to be very, very careful," whispered Aunt Min.

CHAPTER
12

When the Grischer returned to the Library minutes later, she was alone. Eddie and Min missed her entrance entirely. No *KA-BANG* of the Library door. No *THUD, THUD, THUD* of her feet.

Suddenly she was just there. Sitting in the Librarian's chair. Eddie watched her take a phone from her bag. Sunshine from the skylight reflected off her glasses. He couldn't see her eyes.

"Get down," whispered Min from behind. "Think of that poor fly!"

Eddie gulped and dropped low.

They heard beeps. Then a faint ring.

"Hello, Robert?" said the Grischer. "It's me. Estelle."

"Her brother," whispered Min. "The superintendent."

"Yes," said the Grischer. "I'm here at Ferny Creek— and not a moment too soon. You're right, this library's a money pit. It's glassed in like a terrarium. No wonder the heating bills are so high. The sooner we get these windows blocked off, the better."

Min gripped Eddie's leg tightly.

"The Principal?" said the Grischer. "Not a problem. He's making whiny noises, of course. Everyone loves the library, boohoo. He even went on about the view. Puh! What do these kids need with a view? Did *we* have a view? Did *we* have Winnie-the-Pooh and nursery rhymes?"

There was a long moment of silence.

"Don't worry, I can handle the Principal. I'll start by weeding the book collection. That won't be hard. Almost every book in here is a weed. I'll clear them out gradually. He won't even notice."

Min shuddered.

The Grischer was listening to her brother again.

"I agree, Robert," she answered. "This room

is perfect—bigger than any of the others we've looked at. With the windows blocked off and the books cleared out, it will make an excellent testing center for your new district testing program. All we need really are tables and chairs. On days when there's no testing, we'll turn off the heat and lights. Save a lot of money."

The Grischer said good-bye and put away her phone. There was a tiny squeak of the chair as she stood up, then a *click* at the door. Other than that, her departure was silent.

"At least we know the worst," said Min, her voice shaky. "The Grischers are going to close the Library."

"Really? Can they do that?" Eddie was hoping he had misunderstood.

"Yes, they can. They're being sly with Mr. Steadman, but that's the plan. They're going to turn this wonderful room into . . . a testing center. Most of the time, it will be empty. Dark, cold, and empty."

"No books?" said Eddie.

"No books." Aunt Min gazed upward. "The

skylight will go, too. The story-time chair, the comfy couch, the story-time carpet. Even the windows. Everything will go."

Eddie tried to think of something to say.

But he couldn't.

When the Grischer returned, just a short while later, she was carrying a large cardboard box. Eddie wondered what it was for.

Then, suddenly, he got it.

"Hide!" he yelled. Grabbing his aunt, he half pushed, half carried her to the back of the tray.

Clinging together, they watched as the pale fingers began clearing off the desk. Things disappeared into the cardboard box. The bobbing duck. The photo. The bowl of golden stars.

And then—as Eddie and Min watched in horror—the Grischer reached for their tray.

"Hang on!" cried Min.

Up went the tray with a sickening lurch. Eddie was thrown backward. He landed on his aunt.

At that moment, a cheerful voice called from

the doorway. "Are you expecting us?"

The tray hovered, tilting at a perilous angle. Eddie and Min clung desperately to the side.

"We're Kindergarten B," said the voice. "It's our book exchange time!"

The tray wobbled. Eddie and Min slid wildly into the loose papers. Then down went the tray—*BANG!*—back onto the desk.

"Bring the children in," said the Grischer. "Are their hands clean?"

"Oh, Aunt Min, this is terrible." Eddie's head was in a spin. "We're in such big trouble!"

"Courage, Eddie, this is no time to lose heart. We need a new hiding place, quickly! Before she comes back."

After a hurried discussion, they agreed that Eddie would go on a scouting mission.

So once again he stepped into the open, alone. His huge eyes gleamed. His antennae explored the air. Where were the kindergartners? More important, where was the Grischer? Not only was she hard to see and hear, she was also crafty and scheming. Plus, she obviously *hated* bugs. A deadly combination.

There! She was busy with the children in the picture book area. Eddie could focus on his mission—a new, safe hideout, close enough for Min to walk to.

A voice in his head said, "Impossible!"

He glanced around. Nothing on the desk would work. The Grischer was going to dump all the Librarian's possessions into the cardboard box, and who knew where that box would end up?

They needed a place that the Grischer wouldn't notice. . . .

There was a drawer.

It was small and narrow, in the front of the desk, facing the Librarian's chair. And it was open— not very wide, just a crack—but wide enough for a bug to slip through. Eddie darted inside.

He looked around. The drawer was shallow, and clearly it hadn't been used much. Nothing there but a few pencil stubs, an old dried-up pen, and a cotton ball. Plus the usual pad of yellow stickies.

Looking good, thought Eddie.

But not perfect.

The Grischer might open the drawer to clean it.

He crawled to the rear of the drawer. There appeared to be extra space behind a wooden divider. He peeked over . . . and there it was. A secret compartment. Or maybe not exactly secret. But there was certainly a separate little section at the very back of the drawer. It was partly covered by a piece of wood that could act, if you happened to be extremely small, as a roof.

Eddie allowed himself one quick "Yes!"

CHAPTER
13

"Perfect!" said Min when she saw the secret compartment of the drawer. "Exactly what we need."

Eddie smiled.

It had been hard to hide his fear as he helped Min to the drawer. She was woefully slow, and the desktop was much more exposed now with so many things removed. Remembering the unfortunate fly, Eddie had to stop himself from yelling "HURRY!" as she tottered along.

"I feel so much safer here," she said as she settled in. "Quite cozy, really. The little roof makes it almost like a house." Perched on the cotton ball that Eddie had fetched from the front of the drawer, she looked surprisingly comfortable.

"We even have a bit of light," said Eddie.

Beneath the "roof" of the secret compartment, there was a thin crack that allowed light in. It was only, as Eddie said, a *bit* of light, because even the main drawer opening wasn't large. But for bugs with night vision, it was enough.

"Couldn't be better," said Min. "I'm a very lucky bug."

It wasn't long before they *both* felt grateful for the drawer. When the kindergartners left, the Grischer started cleaning the huge desk in earnest. It was as if she were trying to erase all memory of Ms. Laurel. The air grew thick with sprays and cleansers. But hidden away in their secret compartment, Eddie and Min were spared the worst.

"Come sit," said Aunt Min, patting a spot beside her cotton ball. "I'll tell you a story."

"A book story?" asked Eddie.

Min nodded. "Have I ever told you about *The Borrowers*?"

"Who are they?"

"Tiny people," said Min, "who live under floors and behind walls in the houses of the big Squishers."

"Ooh," said Eddie, already entranced. "Are they as tiny as us?"

"Not quite," said Min.

"Do they squish?"

"Goodness, no. The Borrowers understand what it's like to be little, even if they look like Squishers."

"Why do they live under the floor?"

Min sighed. "Can't you guess? They hide from the Squishers, just as we do. And like us, they are often in danger. All they want, really, is a safe home."

"Ooh," said Eddie again. "I wish I could read that book."

"It's here in the Library," said Min. "For *now*, anyway. But listen! I can tell you some of it."

So she told Eddie about the time the Borrowers were imprisoned by some nasty Squishers in an attic, and the only way to escape was by balloon.

It was a small adventure, like the Borrowers themselves. But for a reader of Eddie's size, it was perfect.

Time passed quickly. Min had just finished her story when the last school bell rang. *BRRRRRING!*

"Good," said Min. "Let's hope you-know-who will *leave* now!"

And as if she had heard, the Grischer slipped away almost immediately. There was barely a *click* of the door.

The moment she was gone, Eddie boosted Min up the front panel of the drawer. Together the two bugs looked out.

The top of the desk was unrecognizable.

"There's nothing left!" said Eddie.

An empty expanse of wood lay before them. Nothing but ink blotches, tea stains, and the dents and scars of librarians past. Not one single item to remind them of Ms. Laurel. Only the huge, dark computer remained, looming above the desk.

Aunt Min stared at the desk in dismay. "Oh, my."

Then her gaze moved slowly toward the bookshelves, and her expression grew sad. Eddie knew what she was thinking. She was imagining the books gone, too—and with them, all their secret worlds.

For a long time, she stared out at Library, still and quiet. Then, as Eddie watched, she reached into the room with her antennae. Her whole body quivered, and from deep inside came a low mournful thrum.

"Aunt Min?" said Eddie after a while. "What are you doing?"

"Just . . . feeling it. Sensing. Remembering. Wishing I could walk through the Library one last time."

Glancing at her nephew, she shook her head. "Oh, Eddie, I wanted *you* to feel it, too."

"Feel what?"

"The magic." She looked around again.

Suddenly she stamped a tiny foot.

"I don't understand!" she cried, her voice

hoarse. "It makes me so mad! How *foolish* these Squishers are to close a library! Where will the children go to find stories? To experience, with their own eyes and ears and minds, the greatest adventures ever imagined? Oh, Eddie, I've spent such thrilling hours in this room. I've *seen* the magic. Where will the reading magic happen if there's no Library?"

He could only nod.

"I feel so helpless," continued Min. "How I wish I had a voice loud enough for that Grischer to hear. Wouldn't I give her a piece of my mind! Wouldn't I tell *her* a thing or two!"

"I'd love to see that," said Eddie.

And for a moment, he could actually picture it— Aunt Min giving the Grischer a brisk scolding, telling her in no uncertain terms about books and libraries, and why they were important.

"Ah, well." Suddenly Min sagged. "Silly dream, isn't it? Who'd listen to an old bug like me? Are you hungry, dear?"

As soon as she said it, Eddie realized that he

was very hungry indeed. It had been a long time since his last meal. He scooted down the desk leg, looking for dinner.

There wasn't any! The longer he looked, the more surprised he grew. Yes, there had been only one class today, but there were always at least a couple of children with food dribbling out of their pockets—even if it was just yesterday's cookie. It wasn't till he glanced at the walls that he understood.

The Library posters were gone. The ones that said "READ!" with pictures of dogs wearing glasses, or dinosaurs tucked into bed, or famous Squisher athletes — all reading books. In some places, there was nothing but a bare spot and tiny pinholes. But here and there, a new sign had been put up.

FOOD-FREE ZONE!
THIS MEANS YOU!

Clearly, the Grischer was serious about her no-food rule. All Eddie could find was a dried-up piece of cough drop that had been stepped on at least five times.

"Gag," said Min when she saw it.

"It was stuck to the floor," said Eddie.

"I can tell. Sorry, dear. I know you did your best."

"It's just not the same out there, Aunt Min."

"I know. Never mind, I have an idea."

"Tell me," said Eddie.

"You'll have to wait till the Cleaner moves through. But after that, if you promise to stay out of trouble—"

"I do!"

"You can go to the teachers' room."

"The teachers have their own room?"

"Yes. They go there when they want a rest from the children. They sit and talk and eat."

"Eat?" said Eddie. "YAY!"

Now that he had a meal to look forward to, it was hard to wait. But he could already hear the *rrrrrumble* of the Cleaner's cart coming down the hall. This was followed very quickly by the *KA-BANG* of the Library door opening. Soon the vacuum let out a *ROARRRR* and began its work.

"Just one more thing," said Min when the noise finally died away.

"What?" said Eddie.

"There could be a mouse in the teachers' room."

"A mouse? Are you kidding? You mean, like Stuart Little?"

"I wish," said Min. "No, a *real* mouse. A wild mouse."

"WHAT?" said Eddie.

"Well . . . probably not. Listen, I shouldn't have mentioned it. I heard some teachers talking, but that was weeks ago. I'm sure it's gone by now."

"Really?"

"Yes, really. Listen, the Cleaner's leaving the building. Are you ready?"

"Aunt Min? You're sure about the mouse?"

"Eddie! Stop worrying. Go!"

Well, as you learned just a few pages ago, when someone told Eddie to "stop worrying," it had pretty much the *opposite* effect on him. The walk to the teachers' room was long. By the time he got there, he felt deeply uneasy. After all, a mouse is no small matter! Or rather, it *is* a small matter . . . but not if you're the size of a button yourself.

Eddie stood outside the teachers' room, wavering. Fear ordered him to retreat. Hunger begged him to—please, please, please—go find some dinner.

Hunger won.

The door to the teachers' room was closed, but there was a generous gap between the door and the floor. After a few last worrisome thoughts in which a mouse's front teeth featured prominently, Eddie slipped under the door.

Almost immediately, he smelled food. Even in the middle of the night, even after vacuuming, the teachers' room smelled wonderfully tasty. Eddie had never encountered so many interesting odors at once.

Could one of those smells be . . . mouse?

There were tables in the teachers' room and lots of chairs. Up against the wall stood a long black leather couch, bigger than the one in the

Library but not as comfy looking. A tiny light had been left on over the sink. Eddie took it all in, wondering how carefully the Cleaner had vacuumed this room.

Not very, it turned out. Thinking about it, Eddie wasn't surprised. The Cleaner was tall and had no antennae, not even short ones. So of course he couldn't sense what Eddie could sense. The area under the couch, for example. Eddie could tell that the Cleaner had not pushed his vacuum cleaner *there* in a very long time.

"Wow!" said Eddie. He crept forward.

The under-couch zone was magnificent! A vision of plenty such as he'd never seen. Over here, a sweet green pea. There, a chunk of carrot. A blueberry, a fuzzy piece of cheese. Chocolate cookie crumbs everywhere! There was even a bit of liver sausage which, being a vegetarian, Eddie walked right past.

In the end, he chose the blueberry. It was huge, but as he had already learned from his raisin, roundish things were easy to roll. Even more

important, the berry was juicy and plump. Eddie
knew it would be delicious.

Aunt Min loves fruit, he thought, pushing the
blueberry across the room. This was going to be
great!

It was a bit of a squeeze, getting the berry under
the door. But out in the hallway, it rolled very well.
So well, in fact, that it started to roll away.

"Stop!" cried Eddie as it made a break for a
classroom.

"Slow down!" he yelled as it barreled past the
Library door.

Eventually, he got it into the Library. He pushed it deep under the librarian's desk—far from the edges where it might be seen, and away from where the Grischer would put her feet. There were some cords under there that belonged to the computer, but he managed to get around them. The light was dim, but even so, as Eddie parked his berry, he spotted something he hadn't noticed before.

A pad of yellow stickies.

"Hah!" muttered Eddie. It must have fallen off the desk. He felt heartened to see that *something* still remained of the Librarian—here, as well as in the drawer. She certainly did love stickies!

Steadying the berry with his front feet, Eddie dug right in. He chomped firmly into it with his mandibles, gobbling down his own dinner before carving out a large chunk for Aunt Min. The berry tasted every bit as delicious as it looked. Purple juice dripped from his jaws, thorax, and feet.

Maybe I shouldn't have chosen something so

messy, thought Eddie. Glancing at his front feet, he realized that he must be marking the floor with footprints.

Thank goodness he had noticed. The Grischer would be sure to spot a blueberry-juice trail on her desk.

He walked over to the yellow pad and wiped his feet on the top sticky till they were dry. Then he peered at the paper, leaning in so close that his eyes almost touched it. Yes, just as he'd expected, little blue marks all over.

He picked up the blueberry chunk and started to climb the desk leg. As usual, his mind wandered. It went searching for something more interesting than the long, slow slog up the desk.

He was halfway up when it happened. A shock ran through him that was so strong, he got chills.

"Wow!" he said.

Eddie had a *great* idea!

CHAPTER
14

A great idea is an extraordinary experience in anyone's life—bug or Squisher. And if you are ever lucky enough to have such an experience, it would be wise to consider your timing.

Try not to have *your* great idea, as Eddie did, while struggling up a sheer precipice, hauling an enormous, awkward lump of dripping fruit. He got so excited, he almost fell.

"Aunt Min!" he cried when he got to the drawer. "Aunt Min!"

With his mandibles full of blueberry, it came out like this: "Amm-mmm! Amm-mmm!"

He dropped the chunk into the drawer and scuttled down behind.

"Is that really blueberry?" Min rushed over. "Yes! I could smell it. My favorite!"

"What?" said Eddie. "You said you liked raspberry best."

"Raspberry's my *other* favorite. I just—"

"Never mind, doesn't matter. Aunt Min, I have a great idea!"

"Eddie, sweetheart, this berry is beyond words. So ripe, so juicy."

"No," said Eddie. "I mean, yes. I mean, no. Aunt Min, listen. *That's* my idea. Blueberry juice!"

Min was attacking her meal with great zeal, but she glanced up politely. "You're going to have to be more specific. How is blueberry juice an idea?"

"It's like ink," he said. "Like the ink on a stamp pad. If we still had the Librarian's stamp pad, we could use that. But the stamp pad is gone now, so we'll have to use blueberry juice instead."

"Eddie, *what* are you talking about?"

"We can write a message, Aunt Min. With *juice*! A message to the Grischer. We can give her a piece of your mind. Like you said."

Min stopped chomping. "Write?" she repeated in confusion. "Eddie? Can you . . . *write?*"

A thrill ran through Eddie. "I don't know . . . can I?"

Min's eyes were so big, they looked ready to pop. "Eddie, I have to tell you, I have never . . . not in all my born days . . . ever heard of a bug who could write."

Eddie thought about this. But it made no sense. "Why not? I can *read*, can't I? Why shouldn't I write, too?"

Min, who had forgotten all about eating, pushed the berry chunk aside. "Well, I . . . golly . . . I mean, who'd ever think . . ." Almost too flummoxed to speak, she stammered, "Eddie . . . now, dearest . . . even if you *could* write . . . what would you write *on?*"

Eddie smiled. "Stickies!"

"Stickies?" repeated Min. "You mean . . . those little yellow papers?"

She squinted into the gloom at the pad of stickies that had been lying in the drawer since they arrived.

Eddie nodded. "Yes, those. There's another pad under the desk."

It didn't seemed possible that Min's eyes could get bigger, but they did. "You want to write . . . on those stickies?"

"Yes!" said Eddie. "I want to write on the stickies, using blueberry juice as ink. I know I can make marks, Aunt Min. I already did it by accident. My foot can be a *pen*!"

Min sat down with a plop. "Eddie, I am totally gobsmacked. I don't know whether you're the smartest bug who ever crawled or . . . or . . . as wacky as a bedbug."

Eddie laughed. "Maybe I am wacky. But I really want to try. I can at least *try*, can't I?"

Before she could answer, he continued. "It's like that story about the cows that typed. How did they know they could type if they didn't try?"

Min laughed. "Well . . . yes. But Eddie, that was a make-believe story."

"Yeah, well, I'm making up a story, too," said

Eddie. "And in *my* story, I'm making believe I can *write!*"

He stamped his front foot for emphasis.

Min's cackle filled the drawer. "Eddie, you're one in a million. Yes, of course, anything's possible. You must go ahead and try."

"Great!" said Eddie. "I'm ready to start!"

"Maybe so," said Min. "But I think you'll have to wait."

She pointed up. Dark clouds had rolled across the sky. They blocked the moonlight and were starting to send raindrops onto the skylight with a sharp *rat-a-tat*. The pad of stickies was now almost invisible.

"Rats!" said Eddie. He hated waiting. He was *so* ready to be a writer.

"Never mind," said Min. "Morning will come soon."

But it didn't. Morning seemed to take a whole week. Eddie paced their small space restlessly.

"Relax," said Min. "You're as jumpy as a grasshopper."

It was true. He was practically vibrating. To calm himself, he began to do some practicing. Of course, he couldn't actually write anything. But it wasn't hard to imagine making letters— the lovely swirls of an *s*, the jagged lines of a *z*. He remembered watching the children write in Room 19—the way they held their pencils and moved them across the paper. All night long, using his right front foot, Eddie formed letters in the air, mimicking the movements of the children while his aunt snoozed nearby.

Just before dawn, the rain stopped. As the first light crept into the drawer, Eddie assembled his tools.

The berry chunk.

The stickies.

His foot.

"What are you going to write?" asked Min.

Eddie smiled. "I thought *you* might know. You said you wanted to talk to her, Aunt Min. The Grischer. You wanted to give her a piece of your mind. What would you say if you had the chance?"

"Well," said Aunt Min, "the first thing I'd say is—leave this Library alone! I'd say that I need books to read, and so does Eddie, and so do reading bugs everywhere. And so do the children, by the way. Those children are hungry for stories—I've seen that day after day!—and what are you *thinking*, robbing them of stories and giving them tests instead? I'd tell her that books are *exactly* what children and bugs need. They're good for reading, yes, but they're also good for touching and smelling and turning the pages, and cuddling up on, and sharing."

She paused, panting loudly.

"Aunt Min?

"Yes?"

"That was great."

"Thank you, Eddie."

"But I think it's . . . er . . . a bit long."

"Oh," she said. "I suppose it *is* a lot to ask of blueberry juice and a sticky."

He nodded.

"Well then, Eddie, put it in your own words.

You'll know what to say."

Eddie took a deep breath.

He dipped a front foot in the juice and swooshed it around till it was good and wet. Then, holding his foot high, he used his other legs to climb onto the sticky pad.

He stared at the big yellow square. Where to start?

Top-left corner, he decided. Just like for reading.

Reaching out with his juice-covered foot, he placed it on the sticky. Slowly, he dragged it down.

It worked! He was making a line!

Then he stopped. Stared.

"Aunt Min, it's not right. The line is too thin!"

No use pretending. Eddie's line was a poor, weak thing. Almost invisible. Far too pale for a Squisher to read.

"Your foot is very tiny," Min reminded him. "Why don't you try again? With *two* feet."

Eddie dipped both front feet in the blueberry

chunk and tried again. He wiggled backward to take a look.

"Better!" said Min. "Much better."

Eddie agreed. And if two feet worked better, then three might be better still. Or four? Balancing on his two back feet, Eddie dipped all his other feet into the blueberry chunk . . . and promptly fell over!

Min smiled. "Two feet seems best for writing. But it never hurts to experiment."

"Did you see me, Aunt Min?" said Eddie. "I was standing on *two legs*. Like a Squisher! Here, I'll do it again. I'm a Squisher, see? I'm a Squisher."

As Eddie balanced on his two back legs, he and his aunt laughed heartily.

"How do the Squishers do it?" said Min. "Wobbling along that way. They look as though they should topple over."

"Maybe their feet keep them up," said Eddie. "Their feet are huge."

"Good golly, yes. Imagine having those big floppy feet!"

"Imagine having *six* of those feet!"

At that, they both rolled about, laughing.

But as Eddie settled onto all his legs again, he couldn't help feeling sorry for the Squishers. What a nuisance it must be, having to keep your balance all the time.

"Eddie?" said Min.

"Yes?"

"Your sticky?"

"Oh. Right." Eddie returned to his task. Using his two front feet to write, he added a round shape to the line he had made, so that it looked like this:

P

"That's a *p*," cried Aunt Min. "Eddie! You're doing it! You're actually writing!"

"More juice," said Eddie.

Concentrating hard, he printed two more letters.

Ple

"*Ple?*" said Aunt Min. "I don't understand. What's *ple?*"

"I'm not finished," said Eddie.

And he wasn't. But new as he was to writing, he had already figured something out. Writing took a long time. And it took up a *lot* of space on the sticky.

He glanced up at the light, shining in now through the drawer opening. It was brighter every minute. Soon the Squishers would arrive.

"I may not be able to write the whole message now," he said.

"Oh, Eddie darling," said Aunt Min. "Don't you see? This is *already* a miracle! A bug writing a message."

"It's not a message *yet.*" He plunged his feet back into the chunk.

As quickly as he could, he added three more letters. An *a*. An *s*, which was the trickiest of all, so far. And finally, another *e*.

"There," said Eddie.

His word pretty much filled the sticky.

Please

Aunt Min stared at it. "Please? Your first word is *please*?"

"Yes," said Eddie. "Is that okay?"

"Well, *please* is a fine word. But I don't know. Please? To the Grischer?"

"Why not? I'm asking for something."

"Well . . . yes."

"And you know what Pa always says."

"What?"

"He says that everyone has a soft spot under their shell. I'm saying 'please' to her soft spot."

Min was silent a moment. Then she started to laugh.

"What can I say? You're a better bug than me, Eddie. *Please* is the perfect choice for your first word."

"Gee," said Eddie, "thanks!"

"So what's next?"

"I'm going to stick this sticky onto one of the Library books—where the Grischer will see it and read it. Then I'll write another word, and another, and another. I'll stick them *all* on books. Little by little, she'll get the message."

"Good plan," said Min. "Which book?"

"I thought *you* might have an idea. You know everything about the Library."

"Not everything," said Min. "But I think I know a good book for your sticky."

"Which one?"

"It's about a bug," she said. "Well, sort of. It's called *The Very Hungry Caterpillar*. It's about a caterpillar who eats and eats. And everything he eats makes a hole in the book! Isn't that clever? The children can poke their fingers through the holes."

Eddie grinned. "Sounds great. Where can I find it?"

Aunt Min gave him directions. "You'll have to hurry. It's almost time for school to start."

Eddie took a deep breath. It had been a long night. The thought of yet another trek was daunting.

But the sooner the Grischer got the message, the better.

He stuck the yellow sticky to his back and crawled into the bright morning light.

CHAPTER
15

It wasn't hard to find the C books.

That's where Aunt Min had told Eddie to go. She said that the author of *The Very Hungry Caterpillar* was Eric Carle. "Carle" started with *C*, so the book would be in the *C* section of picture books. Picture books were right beside the story-time carpet. Easy!

What Aunt Min hadn't mentioned was how many *other* authors had names that started with *C*.

Cleaver, Cooney, Crews, Cronin . . .

I'll be here all day, thought Eddie.

But of course, that couldn't happen. A bug with a sticky on his back would be spotted in an instant.

So Eddie started to *run* along the *C* shelf. As he beetled past the books, his eyes skimmed the titles. Was this speed-reading, he wondered? He had heard the Teacher mention such a thing but had never guessed he might actually do it. If his mission hadn't been so important, this speed-reading might be fun.

Then, suddenly, there it was! *The Very Hungry Caterpillar.*

Closed, of course. Tucked among the others. One day, Eddie might be lucky enough to find it open. . . .

For now he focused on getting the sticky off his back. Without Min's help, it was tough. He had to do a lot of grunting, pulling, and twisting before the sticky came free. Then he had to figure out how to attach it to the *book*—without re-gluing it to himself. Lastly, there was the problem of size. The spine of the book was much narrower than the sticky. Eddie had some tricky moments trying to be loyal to the caterpillar hero inside. There were so few insect heroes—the caterpillar book really *did* deserve a sticky all to itself. But in the end, he had to attach the sticky to several other books as well.

And finally, there it was. His first written word. And it was *on a library shelf*! Eddie beamed like a glowworm.

He was walking proudly away along *C* Shelf when . . . he sensed something.

A change.

That's when he heard it—the faint *click* of the Library door being closed, when he hadn't even heard it open.

"Ohmygosh. She's here? Already?"

He turned.

The Grischer moved quickly—from door to desk in a gray-beige blur. Pulling a wet wipe from her purse, she swished it across the desktop, then placed the purse neatly on one corner. Her pale gray coat was hanging on a hook almost before she took it off.

Then she turned.

"Hmm," she muttered. "What's *that*?"

"What's what?" echoed Eddie in his head.

But he knew.

Eric Carle's sticky. She had already spotted it.

Yes. Here she came, charging across the room like an army ant. Before Eddie could react, there she was.

At *C* shelf!

Limbs shaking, he tried desperately to think.

Run?

She'd see him.

But if he stayed where he was, she'd see him anyway.

She snatched up the sticky and raised it to her metal-rimmed glasses. "*'Please'*?" she read out loud.

Slowly, she glanced around the Library. Eddie could see her eyes now. Blue with pink edges. He could hear her suck in her breath.

She spat out a single word.

"*Bug!*"

The pale hands groped wildly—a weapon, a weapon! Eddie watched, still paralyzed, as she snatched up a magazine.

A nanosecond later, it was rolled and in the air. Eddie gasped! He skittered between two books just as the magazine smashed—*THWACK!*—where he'd been standing, frozen.

THWACK! THWACK! THWACK!

Eddie raced to the rear of the shelf and zoomed left.

THWACK!

The space behind him was suddenly empty. *C* books were disappearing! *The Grischer was ripping them off the shelves!*

THWACK!

Eddie ran on. And then—

A hole! At his feet. A tiny gap where *C* shelf and the back of the bookcase didn't meet. Big enough? Eddie jammed himself into the hole. Wriggling hard, he managed, barely, to squeeze through.

He skittered to the shelf below and glanced around. Was this *D* shelf? Wedging himself into a corner, he stopped. Listened.

CRASH! BONK! THUNK! The Grischer was still yanking books off *C* shelf and hurling them to the floor.

He waited. Would she empty *D* shelf next?

"Could I have a word, Ms. Grisch?" Someone had entered the Library.

"Oh, thank you!" whispered Eddie to his rescuer. "Whoever you are, thank you."

He took a long gulping breath. Listening, he heard children's voices as a class arrived. He heard the Grischer greet the new arrivals. He tried to calm himself.

Once again, books helped. Of course, they did.

If a time ever comes in *your* life when you have to hide from an enemy, as Eddie did, and if you happen to be a passionate reader, as Eddie was, then there is no better place to hide in all the world than behind a wall of books. The smell soothed Eddie's raw and jangled nerves. He breathed it in deeply. He leaned hard against the covers. Inside those covers, he knew, there were characters just as frightened as he was—pursued by evil forces, running for their lives, desperate to escape. Anything awful that comes along in life—anything!—has *always* been felt first by a character in a book. Eddie understood this. And even though he couldn't open the books, he was calmed by their presence. Surrounded by stories, he felt less alone.

He didn't *mean* to doze off. Not on a library shelf, for Pete's sake. But it had been such a long night.

He woke up when he heard the word *sticky*. Recognizing the Grischer's raspy voice, he crawled forward between two books and peeked out.

She was facing a group of children on the story-time carpet. Eddie didn't know how old they were, but definitely much younger than the fourth graders in Room 19. The way he could tell (aside from their small size) was this: one was facing backward, two were lying down, and one had its finger up its nose. The Grischer scolded those four and made sure she had everyone's attention before holding up the sticky.

"Does anyone know anything about this?"

Hands flew up.

"Something's written on it," said a child who'd been lying down. "Funny writing. What does it say?"

A child at the front stood up to see better. "It says 'please.' And the writing is skinny. Must have been a teeny-tiny pen."

"A fine-tipped pen!" said another child, jumping up too.

A third child rose. "Or a fancy paintbrush," she said, "with blue ink like my dad uses in his art."

Eddie was thrilled. Not only had they been able to read his writing—they had also complimented his footwork.

More children stood up.

"Sit down!" said the Grischer. "All of you. What I want to know is—*who* put this sticky on the books?"

The children looked around. No hands went up.

The Grischer kept asking questions. Did anyone have blue ink? Did anyone have an extra-fine-tipped pen? Some children had one or the other at home. Nobody recognized the sticky.

All morning, Eddie stayed on *D* shelf. A second class came and went. The Grischer quizzed those children about the sticky, too. Nobody knew where it had come from, of course.

But the children grew ever more curious. Eddie heard them whispering as they walked past his shelf. Fortunately for him, no one was looking for authors whose names began with *D* that morning. Everyone was talking about the mysterious sticky.

"Where did it come from?"

"Why does it say 'please'?"

"Who writes like that? Nobody writes like that."

When the Library finally emptied for lunch—all the children gone, and the Grischer locking the door behind her—Eddie came out of hiding. He ran to Aunt Min as quickly as he could.

"You're alive!" she said, lurching toward him. "For crying out loud, Eddie, you're going to have to stop *scaring* me that way. When I heard her yell 'Bug!' and then all those thwacking noises—"

"I'm fine, Aunt Min."

"Well, good, I'm so relieved. But Eddie, did you hear the children talking? Your sticky's a success."

"Not yet," said Eddie.

That afternoon they stayed snug in their secret compartment. They listened as the Grischer grilled two more classes about the yellow sticky.

"She must have asked everyone by now," said Eddie.

"Everyone except *you*!" said Min.

And somehow they both found that funny. They laughed for a very long time.

CHAPTER
16

At the end of the day, a boy walked into the Library by himself.

"I'm Janek," he told the Grischer. "Mr. Steadman says you need some help? In the Library?"

"Hey," whispered Eddie in the secret compartment. "I know that voice."

"How?" asked Min. "He's not from Room 19."

Eddie and his family knew all the children in Room 19. They might not always recognize faces, and sometimes they forgot names, but they certainly knew the *voices* of the children in their own classroom.

"He's the boy from the hallway," said Eddie. "I told you about him, remember? He came out of the BOYS' ROOM, and he chased away that spider. He saved my life, Aunt Min. He didn't mean to, but he did."

"Well then, bravo, Janek!" said Min. "He's already my friend. Why don't we go closer and listen?"

They crawled to the front of the drawer.

"Hmph!" said the Grischer to Janek. "You're thin as a rail. I said I needed someone *strong* to help with lifting and carrying."

"I'm strong," said Janek.

"Oh, very well," said the Grischer with a sigh. "You can start here. Take all the books in this display and put them into this box. Here's some tape to seal it when you're done."

There was a silence.

"Ms. Grisch?"

"Yes? What is it?"

"Is there something wrong with these books? Do they need to be fixed?"

"No. They're going into storage."

There was another silence, longer.

"Ms. Grisch? These are the graphic novels."

"Yes, I know," said the Grischer. "Comic books. Waste of time."

This time the pause was very long. "Er . . . excuse me, Ms. Grisch, I don't want to be rude . . . but lots of kids love these books."

"Puh!" said the Grischer dismissively. "The students who read graphic novels—and I hope you're not one of them—would be better off working on their math. Do you have any idea how low our math scores are? Compared to other countries?"

"Uh, no, Ms. Grisch. I have not lived here very long . . . and I like math very much. But I also like graphic novels. I like seeing art and story together. Graphic novels are my favorite—"

"Never mind what you *like*," said the Grischer. "The question is—how are your math scores? Are you *good* at math?"

"Yes," said Janek. "I am good at math. Also computers. But books, Ms. Grisch, are—"

"Puh!" said the Grischer again. "Now you *are*

being rude. This conversation is over. Just put the books in the box, if you please, and seal it up. Put the box by the door. When you're done with that section, you can start on this one. Mysteries and thrillers."

"But—"

"Please. No more arguments. Fill and carry, fill and carry, can you do that, Janek?"

"Yes, Ms. Grisch."

After that, there was silence. Nothing but the sound of books dropping into boxes, followed by the *skrawwwwk* of packing tape being pulled.

"Ooooooo," said Min. "She makes my juices boil!"

"Mine, too," whispered Eddie, "and she's too quiet right now. Where *is* she?"

Taking a risk, he peeked out of the drawer. While Janek packed books, the Grischer was doing a slow, careful tour of the Library. She moved at an unusually poky pace, inspecting the books, the shelves, the surfaces. Looking for something.

What?

Eddie was sure he knew. More stickies.

When Janek had packed and stacked six boxes of books, the Grischer sent him away. For a moment, she paused—perhaps in thought. Then she turned to the desk and frowned.

Eddie ducked.

He skittered back to Min. "She's coming!"

There was a sound at the front of the drawer. Eddie and Min looked, then froze in horror.

Fingers!

Long, bony, white—they were *inside the drawer.* Poking. Reaching.

"Ack!" cried Min as a fingernail swept past.

Eddie dragged her quickly out of range.

The fingers retreated. Curling, they gripped the drawer. Then they *pulled.* Hard!

"She's trying to open it," whispered Eddie.

The fingers pulled again. A grinding sound. Wood against wood. The drawer trembled beneath the bugs' feet.

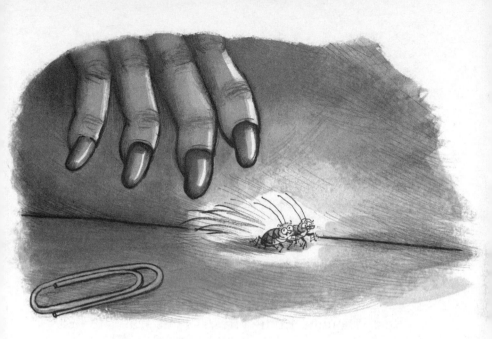

The Grischer grunted, annoyed. "Is there nothing that works in this place?"

The fingers disappeared. A moment later—*BANG!* The whole desk shook! Eddie and Min fell over.

"Ooh!" whimpered Min.

"Are you okay?" said Eddie. "Now she's trying to *shut* the drawer. But look! It barely moved."

He pointed at the opening. Almost the same as before.

They listened. There was a faint *tink*. The hanger.

"She's putting her coat on," whispered Eddie. "Wait."

They listened again, not breathing. Silence. More silence. Finally the sound of her key—

Click.

Eddie turned to his aunt. "She's gone. Are you hurt?"

Min shook her head. "Just shaky. Let's rest a bit."

Rest, thought Eddie. *Rest?* That was the last thing he needed. Tension still raced through his body like electricity through a wire. He had to *do* something!

"Aunt Min?" he said.

"Yes, Eddie?"

"Are you ready for the second sticky?"

CHAPTER
17

Eddie scooted down the desk leg, quivering with excitement. The thought of writing another word made him tingle. Would his blueberry still be waiting under the desk?

It was.

But it looked different. The dusty air had shriveled the berry's surface. It tasted okay when he nibbled, but it wasn't nearly as juicy. Eddie had to chew really hard to get to a good part.

He chomped off the best bit he could find and carried it up to the drawer.

"Have some," he said to Aunt Min.

She took a few bites, then stepped back. "You'll need the rest for your message."

"But you've hardly touched it."

"I'm fine, dear. Go ahead."

So Eddie got to work, soaking his front feet. It took longer to wet them this time, and longer to write the letters.

Aunt Min must have noticed his discouragement.

"Do you know what this reminds me of, Eddie? A book! *Charlotte's Web*. I heard the Librarian read it to third grade. It's about a spider who wrote messages—just like you. Well, not *exactly* like you, of course, with your blueberry juice. Charlotte spun words in her spiderweb."

"That sounds hard," said Eddie.

"I imagine it was very hard. She was trying to save a pig named Wilbur. I remember one of the words she wrote. 'Radiant.'"

"What's 'radiant'?"

"It means shining or glowing. Like you, Eddie, with your green body."

"Really?" Eddie tried the word out in his head. "Radiant. I like it. So what happened to Wilbur?

Did Charlotte save him?"

"I don't know," said Min. "One of the worst moments of my life was when the Librarian told the children to read the rest of the book on their own."

"Oh," said Eddie. "Rotten luck."

"Never mind," said Min. "Here's what I *do* know. *Charlotte's Web* was written by the same Squisher who wrote that book you love—about the mouse. The one you read on the carpet. *Stuart Little*. The author's name is E. B. White."

"Yay," said Eddie. "I'm his number-one fan." He had heard children say that in Room 19.

Aunt Min laughed. "I'll be number two," she said.

With E. B. White for inspiration, Eddie returned to his task with fresh energy. When the Cleaner arrived, Eddie barely paused. Ignoring the ROARRRR of the vacuum, he wrote on.

And finally, there it was. His second word:

save

"Well done," said Min, staring at the sticky. "I like that word a lot. Where do you want to put it?"

"Well, now that you've reminded me about *Stuart*—"

"What a wonderful idea!" said Min. "Yes, put it on *Stuart Little*. You'll find it on *W* shelf. *W* for White. If you hurry, you can get there before dark."

Eddie *meant* to hurry, but he got distracted by the posters. The Grischer must have put up new ones that afternoon. Like the sign that said "Food-free Zone," they had no pictures. Just big letters.

The first had only a single word.

QUIET!

The next poster made him stop and think.

WORK HARDER TODAY THAN YESTERDAY.

"Huh," said Eddie. It wasn't that he disagreed. But he *did* think that in the long run, it might be difficult to keep that up.

The third poster baffled him entirely.

THE HELPING HAND YOU NEED IS AT THE END OF YOUR
OWN ARM.

"Huh," said Eddie again. He read it several times. Maybe you needed hands to understand.

W shelf for novels wasn't easy to find. It was on the bottom of a dark row. By the time Eddie got there, the light was fading. He looked around, disappointed. This spot didn't look nearly important enough for someone like E. B. White.

As he pondered this injustice, the Library suddenly grew darker.

Oh no, thought Eddie. Sundown! He had dawdled too long. Peering anxiously at the books, he saw that most of the titles were impossible to read.

"Nincompoop!" he muttered to himself. After all this trouble, would he have to take the "save" sticky home?

Then, in the next instant, he realized—he didn't have to *see* the book at all.

"Tuna!" he exclaimed as he closed in on *Stuart Little*. His antennae wiggled in recognition—there was no mistaking that fishy aroma. He paused to remember his first happy encounter with this book. The rolling, the reading, the turning of the page—and the oily tuna fish stain on the paper.

It was like meeting an old friend!

Lucky for me, tuna smells so strong, thought Eddie.

Once again, it took some serious wrestling to get the sticky off his back and onto the book. He kept getting parts of his own body—a foot, an antenna—stuck where they weren't supposed to be.

When the sticky was in place, he gave the novel a pat. "There you go, Stuart," he said.

Aunt Min was asleep on her cotton ball when he returned. He crept in quietly. Nestling into the corner he had claimed for himself, he tried to doze off.

But tired as he was, he kept jerking awake. In his dreams, he saw huge outstretched fingers. A terrible voice yelled again and again, "BUG!" as the THWACKS rained down all around. He woke up to find that his legs were moving. Running! Eddie was actually *running* in his sleep!

The next morning he slept in. So did Aunt Min. They were awakened by a loud gasp.

"What?" said Eddie.

"Pah!" said a voice from the bookshelves.

Eddie and Min stared at each other.

The Grischer. *Again* she had caught them off guard! How long had she been wandering the Library while they didn't even know she was there?

"What the—" she said. "WHAT?"

"She's found it," whispered Min. "Your new sticky."

KA-BANG went the door as the Grischer rushed out of the Library. She returned moments later with the Principal.

"I don't understand, Ms. Grisch," said Mr. Steadman. "What's the problem?"

"Right . . . over . . . here!" said the Grischer

tightly. "I left it exactly where I found it. It's evidence. Do you see it? Down *there* with the *W* books?"

"Oh," said the Principal after a pause. "Gosh. Another sticky."

"Exactly! And what are you going to *do* about it?"

The Principal took a moment to answer.

"It just says 'save,'" he replied. "I mean . . . that's harmless, isn't it?"

"Harmless? Harmless? How did it *get* here? That's what I want to know. Who is doing this? I locked the Library door—I'm positive I did! I left late yesterday, and I came in early today. *No children have been in this room*, Mr. Steadman. Is this a practical joke? Is it the cleaning staff?"

"Certainly not," said the Principal. "Mr. Iversen has been cleaning this school for twenty years. He's totally reliable. And not the joking kind, I assure you."

There was a long silence. Eddie and Min stared at each other.

"Do you have any . . . enemies?" asked the Principal. "From another school, perhaps?"

"Enemies!" cried the Grischer. "What are you talking about?"

"Just a thought," said the Principal quickly. "I'm sorry, Ms. Grisch. But it does seem like a small thing to get so upset—"

"It may be small to you," said the Grischer, "but if *you* were the one getting threatening notes—"

"Oh, surely not threatening—"

"Threatening!" repeated the Grischer. "I want you to *do* something about this. I want you to find the perpetrator and—"

"Now, now," said the Principal. "We'll look into it. Why don't you come to the teachers' room and sit down? I believe I saw some Soothing Herbal Tea—"

"Tea?" snapped the Grischer. "Are you seriously suggesting *tea*? Mr. Steadman, I will not be ignored. Kindly find out where these notes are coming from."

"Yes, of course," said the Principal.

There were more sympathetic mumblings as he and Ms. Grisch left the Library.

"Well, I'll be a cross-eyed cockroach!" said Aunt Min. "Did you ever hear such a fuss?"

Eddie shook his head. "Oh, Aunt Min, this is terrible. She doesn't understand at all!"

"She certainly doesn't."

"But I want her to understand. I must have written it wrong."

"You didn't do anything wrong," said Min.

"You just haven't *finished* your message yet. And honestly, anyone who'd get so tumble-tangled over a couple of stickies . . . well, there's just no talking to her."

"But I have to talk to her. I want to reach—"

"I know. Her soft spot. But what if she doesn't *have* a soft spot, Eddie? Have you thought about that? What if she just won't listen?"

Eddie thought for a moment before he answered. "I guess it doesn't matter. I still have to try."

Looking at his aunt, he could see that she wasn't convinced.

"It's like Stuart Little," he said. "Stuart went down a drain. A *drain*, Aunt Min! To get his mother's ring. A Library's more important than a ring. Isn't it?"

Min's face softened. She gazed with longing through the drawer opening.

"Well?" said Eddie.

She sighed. "You've got me there, Eddie. You're absolutely right. Yes, you must finish your message. You must try as hard as you can with your sticky campaign. I'll help you any way I can."

"Thank you," said Eddie.

"And now," said Min, "I think—I hope—we're going to have a treat. Fourth grade should be coming in next. Our very own class from Room 19."

"Really?" said Eddie. "You mean it?"

"Yes! It's their library time."

CHAPTER
18

If you're thinking that the children of Room 19 in Ferny Creek Elementary *knew* Eddie, you'd be wrong. Mr. Patullo's fourth-grade class had not the faintest idea that a small green bug lived behind the old chalkboard on their wall.

But of course, Eddie knew *them*. Day after day, he had listened to every detail of their lives. And now, hearing their voices as they entered the Library, he could hardly keep from rushing out to greet them.

"Wow, Aunt Min! It's so weird to have them here!"

"I know what you mean," said Min. "It discombobulated me too at first."

Eddie was pleased that there was a wonderful word like *discombobulated* to describe how he felt. And if you're not quite sure what it means, imagine this. You are watching a movie in a theater—say, a superhero movie full of thrills and jolts and explosions. Suddenly you look up at that gigantic screen, and you see—your teacher! Yes, it is definitely *her* wearing that metallic silver suit with the red cape blowing in the wind. And yes, she is flying at the speed of sound! It would not be surprising if you felt a bit discombobulated.

That's how Eddie felt when he heard the Room 19 children in the Library. Topsy-turvy. Discombobulated. But he also felt delighted. Listening to the familiar voices, he realized how much he had missed fourth grade.

He remembered something else, too—how much the Room 19 children liked to visit the Library. They chattered happily as they wandered in.

It wasn't long before Sebastian made a discovery.

"Look!" he said from somewhere very near the secret compartment. "A sticky with funny writing on it. Hey everybody, here's another one of those weird messages!"

"Oh, gosh," whispered Min. "Let's get closer."

After their recent experience with the Grischer's fingers, Eddie wasn't sure this was a good idea. But Min was already moving to the front of the drawer.

They peeked out at the fourth graders, who were gathering around the desk.

"What does it say?" asked Josh.

"'Save,'" read Sebastian. "It says 'save.'"

"Save what?" asked Kayla.

Suddenly a shadow fell over the drawer opening, plunging Eddie and Min into darkness.

"What are you doing?" demanded the Grischer. "Who said you could snoop at my desk?"

"I was just passing," said Sebastian. "I just—"

"Ohh!" cried Hazel. "I think I know!"

"Know what?" asked the Grischer.

"Where the stickies are coming from."

"WHAT?" snapped the Grischer. "You tell me

what you mean. Right now!"

Eddie could see the Grischer's face, splotchy and red as she loomed over Hazel. It felt as though she was looming over him, too. He didn't like it!

But Hazel didn't seem bothered at all.

"Wellllllll," she said slowly and with great drama. "Do you know about . . . Miss Cavendish?"

Now all the children were gasping and exclaiming.

The Grischer blinked. "*Who* is Miss Cavendish?"

"She was a volunteer. A long time ago. Back when my mother went to school here. Miss Cavendish was very, very old, and she loved the Library."

Brody interrupted, all excited. "Yeah! My parents talk about her, too. I know about this."

"About what?" demanded the Grischer.

"Wellllllll . . ." said Hazel again, drawing the word out. "One day Miss Cavendish *died*. She just up and died—right in the middle of a story! She was sitting right there, in the story-time chair."

There was a long pause. Eddie knew what the

children were doing. Staring at the rocking chair.

"WHAT?" said the Grischer.

"It's true," said Hazel in her strong, sweet voice. "She just closed her eyes. Like this! They say she had the most beeeeeautiful smile on her face. She loved the Library sooooooo much. And ever since then, people say . . . well, they say she never left! Not really."

"WHAT?" cried the Grischer. "You mean . . ."

"Yes," said Hazel. "A ghost. She's been haunting the Ferny Creek Library for years."

"WHAT?"

Eddie heard something behind him. Her turned to see Aunt Min rolling with laughter on the bottom of the drawer. Her chuckles turned into snorts and squeals. Eddie had to tap her antennae.

"Shh!" he hissed.

Other children were talking now. Apparently they all knew about Miss Cavendish.

"She wants us to *save* something," said Mateo.

"But what?" asked Lily.

Five or six voices answered at once.

"STOP!" cried the Grischer. "All of you! Stop this nonsense right now. There are no such things as ghosts. This is foolishness. You're going to frighten . . ." She looked around, trying to find someone who looked frightened.

But there was no one to point to. Everyone was talking at the same time. The fourth graders seemed to be enjoying themselves quite thoroughly.

Aunt Min was having the best time of all. "This is priceless," she gasped between hiccups.

Eddie didn't understand. "But it's *not* a ghost. It's just me. And some blueberry juice!"

"Of course," said Aunt Min. "Hic! That's what's so funny."

"Well, I don't think it's funny at all. How will the Grischer get the message if she thinks it comes from Miss Cavendish?"

Min laughed again. "Don't you see? It's *better* if the message comes from Miss Cavendish."

Eddie frowned. "Really?"

"Yes, really. She might actually *listen* to a library ghost."

"Oh," said Eddie. "Well . . . that would be good . . . I guess?"

Aunt Min nodded. "That would be very good."

The children meanwhile were still chattering about the famous volunteer. And when they went outside at recess that morning, they talked some more. They must have talked to other children, too. The way Eddie knew was—every class that came into the Library had one thing on their minds. The ghost! Everyone wanted to see the second sticky. Everyone had a story about Miss Cavendish.

The rumors flew like butterflies through Ferny Creek Elementary that day—so many it would be impossible to repeat all of them here. But the following conversation, overheard by Eddie after lunch, will give you some idea of the excitement in the air.

"She died? Here?"

"Yeah! My uncle told me she just dropped forward. Very, very slowly. She didn't even fall off her chair. She was smiling. Uncle Ben said she died happy."

"If she was so happy, why is she haunting the Library?"

"She *likes* it here."

"Yeah, she must like kids."

"Yeah! And books, too."

"Of course she likes books and kids. If she didn't, she'd have volunteered someplace else. Like the animal shelter."

"Well, maybe she did. I heard she had a dog."

"A dog? Really? So do you think there's a ghost *dog*, too?"

"Wow!"

"A ghost with a dog!"

"Yeah! Isn't that awesome?"

"And she's sending us messages? Wow!"

"STOP!" cried the Grischer. "All of you! Stop it at once. That is quite enough."

But they didn't stop. They went on and on. The excitement spread like syrup across a pancake. Eddie got more astonished by the minute.

His new sticky was a sensation!

CHAPTER
19

Eddie was totally dumbfounded by the excitement his stickies had caused. The whole school was buzzing about the Library Ghost. For a while, it was fun to listen. But then he stopped paying attention.

After all, what good did it do? Nothing had changed. The Library was still in danger.

He needed to *finish* his message. But the blueberry was now a dried-up, caved-in mess. First chance he got—the instant school ended—he would head for the teacher's room to find a new berry.

"Absolutely not," said Min. "You know the rules. Not till the Cleaner has been through."

"Aunt Min, pleeease."

She thought for a moment. "Well, I happen to know some very good stories," she said, "for while we wait."

Eddie laughed, realizing that he was being tricked. There was only one way to distract him, and Min knew what it was.

"Okay," he said, finally, "but do you know any more stories about *little* creatures? Like the Borrowers? And Charlotte?"

"As a matter of fact, I do."

And so she told another story. This time the creatures were *extremely* tiny. Smaller than bugs. Much, much smaller.

"They're called Whos," said Min, "and they're so small, they can fit on a speck of dust. A whole village of Whos, Eddie—on one speck of dust."

"Are you making this up, Aunt Min?"

"Oh, no, not me. It's a book, dear, called *Horton Hears a Who!* It's by Dr. Seuss. Horton is the name of an elephant who helps the little Whos."

The story was excellent. It was written in rhyme, and Aunt Min could recite most of it by heart. When it was over, they talked about the Whos for ages while the Cleaner roared through the school.

"I have a favorite sentence in that story," said Min.

"I bet I know," said Eddie. "'A person's a person, no matter how small.'"

"That's the one."

"It's my favorite, too!" said Eddie. "It's one of the smartest things I've ever heard."

Min smiled. "Then we agree."

She waited awhile. Then, "Eddie?"

"Yes?

"You can go to the teachers' room now."

"I can?"

"Yes, of course. The Cleaner's gone home."

"Really?" Eddie had been so absorbed with the Whos, he hadn't even noticed the quiet that had settled over Ferny Creek Elementary.

"Off you go," said Min. "Good luck!"

Eddie shinnied down the desk leg in a light-hearted mood.

"'A person's a person, no matter how small,'" he said out loud. Then he said it again.

It made him feel hopeful. About life. About his berry. The moonlight shone bright through the skylight that evening, and the hallway felt less worrisome. As Eddie hiked to the teachers' room, he got more and more excited. Blueberry or blackberry, either would be fine, but black ink might make a nice change. As for the reddish berries—strawberry, raspberry, cranberry—he wasn't sure they'd be dark enough.

The teachers' room gave off the same rich bouquet of smells as before. Once again the night light glowed over the sink. And once again there was a fine selection of treats laid out beneath the leather couch. Some he recognized from his last visit. Others were fresh.

He searched hopefully among the scraps. A potato chip, a chicken bone, two broccoli heads. A licorice candy. A muffin top. The muffin top had a pale crispy cinnamon surface. Any other time, he would have been thrilled.

But no berry.

Not a berry anywhere.

He let out a sigh of disappointment. Was it possible? Could his entire ink supply have dried up overnight?

And then, in an instant, he forgot about ink.

There was a smell. . . .

Strange. Disturbing. A rank, funky smell.

Food? Had something rotted?

No, he decided as the hairs on his legs slowly rose. Not food. The strange smell was coming from something *else*. Something that didn't belong.

His eyes did a slow, careful scan. Searching for patterns. Watching for movement.

Nothing.

Except a sound so slight, he almost didn't hear it. Something was . . . breathing.

Eddie went still. Every atom in his body tensed. The sound was coming from . . .

The muffin top.

No. Not the muffin top. From behind it.

Peering into the murky stillness, Eddie slowly

made out two dark spots. He stared at them. The spots seemed to stare back.

Eyes.

He peered above and around the eyes. Shapes that had been hidden in the shadows formed. Ears. A pale nose. A sudden flicker . . . whiskers.

The Mouse!

It was *not* Stuart Little. Not by a long shot. This Mouse was wild and dark . . . and big! Eddie felt like Jack in "Jack in the Beanstalk," facing a giant.

What did mice eat? What if a mouse's favorite food was . . . fresh insect?

How fast could a mouse move? Should he run?

These thoughts came and went in a much shorter time than it takes to tell. But then as Eddie stared in terrified befuddlement, something happened.

The Mouse began to nibble at the muffin. Eddie could see the whiskers quiver. And now he could see the pale paws, and the claws gripping the muffin top. *Sharp* claws.

Slowly he backed away, watching the Mouse

every second. The Mouse returned his gaze.

Then Eddie remembered. . . .

Ink.

He couldn't leave until he found some. All he had was "please save."

Eddie stopped moving. He studied the Mouse. He tried to *read* it, the way he would read a book.

The Mouse's gaze stayed locked on Eddie, too. Only its mouth moved. Chewing.

Eddie glanced around the teachers' room. Was there *anything* he could use for ink? Broccoli, potato chip, licorice? A noodle he hadn't noticed before?

He twitched. Glanced back at . . .

The licorice.

Eddie had tasted licorice once. He hadn't liked it. Aunt Min was fond of it, but even she complained about its texture. "Like rubber," she said. "Tasty, but tough as an old boot."

Eddie didn't care about that. As he stared at the piece of licorice, there was only one thing Eddie cared about. Its color. Black.

Black ink would be perfect!

The catch was—the licorice was in a very unfortunate place. Right beside the muffin top.

The Mouse was still nibbling. So far it hadn't paid too much attention to Eddie. But what if Eddie started creeping forward? Would the Mouse understand? What if it thought Eddie wanted to *steal* its muffin top?

He could try a squeak. Mice spoke in squeaks. But it would be so easy to make a mistake. What if Eddie accidentally squeaked something rude like "Gimme that muffin top!"

He decided to whisper instead. Who could object to a whisper? Meeting the Mouse's eyes, he did his best to look humble and polite.

"It's just me," he breathed, almost too softly to hear. "Eddie."

Slowly, he crept forward, staying low. "The muffin top is yours, Mouse," he whispered. "All yours, okay? The only thing I want is that licorice. I'm not even going to eat it. It's for ink. I want to send a message—"

He paused. This was getting *way* too complicated.

The mouse paused, too. It lifted its head and stared at Eddie with growing interest.

Eddie gulped. He began to bargain again, in his tiniest voice. "Just the licorice, Mouse. You can have the potato chip. I bet you like potato chips." He was pretty sure his words weren't going anywhere, but he was hoping his general message would get through.

Slowly he edged closer. . . .

This Mouse really *was* very smelly.

And now Eddie was there—at the licorice. It had an awkward shape. Squarish, but with rounded edges. Rolling it would be complicated.

He heard a sound. *Scritch.* He turned.

The Mouse had moved closer. It was up now on its back legs. *It was standing right in front of Eddie.* The black eyes gleamed. The smell was nauseating.

Desperate, Eddie whispered a final message. "I'm going, Mouse. Just taking my licorice and . . . bye now."

He gave the candy a push. The licorice toppled forward. Eddie followed, pushed again. As he and the licorice passed the broccoli, he looked back.

The Mouse was once again absorbed with its muffin top. Suddenly Eddie felt a huge surge of gratitude to whoever had provided the splendid, crispy, cinnamon-sugary muffin that was keeping the Mouse so busy.

"Thank you!" whispered Eddie to the unknown teacher.

It took a ridiculously long time to cross the room. The licorice was even worse than the blueberry. It had a mind of its own and never once went where Eddie wanted it to go. At long last he reached the door. He paused to look back at the shadowy hulk of the couch. In the pale glow of the night light, all was still.

Eddie's relief was so strong, he felt giddy. Even generous.

"Good luck, Mouse," he called as loud as he could.

CHAPTER
20

Eddie's licorice continued to be uncooperative all the way back to the Library. It tumbled every which way as Eddie pushed.

"You're going to be *ink!*" he told the candy several times as he wrestled it down the hall. Without these reminders, he might have just given it a good kick and walked away in disgust. By the end of his journey, he was extremely annoyed with that licorice.

When he finally reached the desk, he was worn to a frazzle. No way could he carry this candy to the top. He bit off a large chunk and saw to his relief that, when chewed and mixed with digestive juices, the licorice *did* produce a sticky black substance. He hauled the soggy chunk up the desk and collapsed at the top.

"Eddie? Is that you?" called Min from the drawer.

"Be right there!" Leaving his burden behind, he staggered to the drawer and dropped in.

"What's that smell?" asked Min.

"Licorice."

"Licorice! Good golly, did you run into Willy Wonka?"

Eddie knew about Willy Wonka, of course. He was the candy man in the story of *Charlie and the Chocolate Factory*. But struggling with the licorice for so long had put him in a grumpy mood.

"No," he replied. "I did *not* meet Willy Wonka. If you really want to know, I met a big, stinky mouse."

"What? Oh, Eddie! You met—the Mouse?"

"Yes," he replied. "Up close. Closer than I wanted."

So then, of course, he had to tell the whole story. He described the Mouse in detail. He even imitated its bold gaze and twitching whiskers.

"How lucky that it was eating a muffin top!" said Aunt Min.

"It wasn't *just* the muffin top," said Eddie. "It was me, too. I think I may have calmed that Mouse down. I just kept looking it in the eye."

"You tamed it, Eddie. Like Max with the Wild Things." Min took a breath and recited from memory, "He 'tamed them with the magic trick of staring into all their yellow eyes without blinking once.'"

"Yes!" said Eddie. "That's exactly how it was. Except the Mouse's eyes were black, not yellow. But you're right, I didn't blink. Not even once."

Aunt Min laughed. "You *can't* blink, Eddie. You're a bug."

"Oh," said Eddie. "Yeah. Right!"

He laughed too. And as usual when the two of them found something particularly funny, they fell on their backs and rolled around, cackling and hooting.

Finally Eddie stood up. "Time to make ink,

Aunt Min. And listen, I have an idea—why don't we go up top? Onto the desk? There's nobody here now. I could boost you."

"Could you? Oh, that would be splendid! I've had such cabin fever."

"What's cabin fever?"

"Just . . . well . . . a feeling of being trapped. You *know* I'm not the kind of bug who can stay cooped up."

"I know," said Eddie. "Come on then."

He fetched a blank sticky from the yellow pad and fastened it to his back. A minute later, they were both standing on the desk.

"YAHOOOO!" crowed Min. "Isn't the moonlight fine?"

And indeed, a full moon beamed through the skylight, straight onto the desk. The sky sparkled with stars.

"Glorious," said Min. "And there's your licorice."

"Right," muttered Eddie as he unfastened his sticky. "Might as well get started."

Making licorice ink turned out to be even

worse than he'd imagined—a miserable, tedious ordeal. With blueberry juice, the "ink" was already there. With licorice, he had to chew.

After five minutes, he *hated* the taste of licorice.

He chewed for hours, and he had to return twice to the floor for more chunks. Min tried to help with the chewing, but to her, licorice was a treat, so she kept swallowing it instead of spitting it out. Also, she tired quickly. It was easier to do it himself.

The moon offered enough light—just barely—to write. But it wasn't till dawn that Eddie managed to finish his message:

the library

Two words. *Two,* this time! He was so happy, he could have burst.

"*Please save the library,*" said Aunt Min, looking as proud as Eddie felt. "Is that your whole message?"

"Yes."

"I love it. Perfect."

"Thank you," said Eddie. "Do you want to

decide where it goes?"

Min looked pleased. "It's the last sticky, so it should go in the most special place. Do you know that tall red cabinet at the back, Eddie? The one that's so beautifully carved?"

"You mean—your favorite cabinet? With all the other colors?"

"Yes! Miss Cavendish *gave* that cabinet to the Library. She made it herself. Imagine!" Min clapped her front feet in admiration. "And isn't that fitting! Because on top of Miss Cavendish's cabinet—that's where you'll find the *little* books."

"Little? Like us?"

Min nodded. "Tiny books, just right for a child's small hands—or a bug's small feet. One is called *Little Fur Family*. Another is *The Tale of Peter Rabbit*. And there's a special box that holds four little books by Maurice Sendak. The Nutshell Library. One of them is my all-time favorite. *Chicken Soup with Rice*. I would so love it if you could put the last sticky on that book. Are you up for a climb?"

Eddie had already had more than enough

exercise for one night. But what could he do? The book was Min's all-time favorite.

"Sure," he said.

Miss Cavendish's cabinet was at the opposite end of the Library—another long hike. The sky grew lighter as Eddie trudged slowly across the great expanse of floor, wearing his sticky like a big floppy roof.

Out of the corner of his eye, he spotted the story-time carpet, but he turned away. This was no time to be tempted by an open book! He was glad, too, that the sticky hid the posters from his view. No matter how odd or boring the Grischer's new posters were, he couldn't help but read them—it was just so amazing that words could be on walls as well as in books.

When he reached the cabinet, he discovered a problem. The cabinet's surface was shiny and slippery. Tricky to get up.

Eddie shrugged and started to climb. By this point, not even glass would have stopped him.

Twice on his way up, he slipped—heart-stopping

drops that sent him plummeting nearly to the floor. His third try got him more than halfway.

That's when, almost too faint to hear . . .

Click!

The tiniest sound. Barely there.

Except it was.

A key, opening the Library door.

Eddie paused, holding his breath.

The Grischer!

He turned to look, but the sticky blocked his view.

He concentrated hard, using his whole body to sense her. Listening. Smelling. Feeling the air. He could tell when she reached her desk. Yes. There. The soft *tink* of the hanger on the hook.

Silence.

He waited, hardly daring to breathe. There he clung, fully exposed, with a bright yellow sticky on his back:

the library

This time, there would be no hiding.

His only hope was distance—he was a long way from the desk. Maybe she would stay where she was. Maybe children would come. A teacher. Oh, please, thought Eddie.

He stayed still. He ached with the effort of holding on.

Then suddenly, she was *there*.

So close, Eddie could feel her body heat. So close, he could smell the breakfast on her breath! Bacon. Burned toast.

And in that instant, Eddie knew, beyond a doubt, what the Grischer was doing. She was *reading* the yellow sticky.

He heard a gasp.

All this time, through long days and dark nights, through terrible dangers and difficulties, Eddie had managed to stay calm.

But even a bug has his limits.

He let out a thin bleat of fear. The kind that would never normally be heard by a great big Squisher. Not unless the room was very, very quiet. Not unless the Squisher had excellent hearing.

In this fateful moment, both those things were true.

"What?" said the Grischer. "Did somebody . . . *say* something?"

Eddie couldn't stop himself. He bleated again.

"What?"

He thought of the rolled-up magazine. He remembered the *THWACK* as it hit. Suddenly he panicked. He began to *run* like the dickens up the cupboard.

The Grischer didn't move. Just stood like a statue and stared. And of course if you think about it, you will know that she wasn't seeing Eddie at all.

She was watching a small yellow sticky as it raced up a tall red cabinet—entirely on its own. A sticky that had just *talked* to her!

All Eddie heard were the thuds.

THUD! THUD! THUD! THUD! THUD! THUD! THUD!

The sound of her big Squisher feet as she crossed the Library and ran—

KA-BANG!

Out the door.

CHAPTER 21

When Eddie reached the top of Miss Cavendish's cabinet, he did what he had come to do. He found the Nutshell Library—four little books in a box—and planted his sticky across them. He made sure to press extra hard on *Chicken Soup with Rice.*

The Nutshell books looked wonderful! They stood in a row of other small books, propped up by wooden squirrels on each side. Eddie loved that the books were so close to bug size.

He was still admiring them when children's voices sounded at the door.

Eddie ran behind one of the squirrels and

peeked out. Three children were standing on the story-time carpet.

"Nobody's here," said a boy with glasses. "We beat Ms. Grisch."

"Good!" said a girl with ribbony braids. She walked straight to the story-time chair and pointed.

"There!" she said. "*That's* where it happened."

"Well, go ahead," said the third child, a boy with red hair. "Sit on it!"

"Think I won't?" said the girl. "Look! Here I am. *Sitting.* In Miss . . . Cavendish's . . . chair!"

As for what happened next, well, it may have been the result of some movement the girl made without thinking. Suddenly, the chair just . . . dropped backward!

The girl leaped to her feet with a squeal. Behind her, the chair rocked madly.

"Your turn!" squeaked the girl to the boy with glasses.

He took a quick step back. Then he glanced around uneasily. "Hey!" he said. "That cabinet

down there matches this chair. It's got the same carving and paint."

"Hey, yeah," said the other boy. "And look! Wow, you guys! Up there. Can you see it?"

"I don't believe it!" said the girl, clapping her hands to her face. "It's a new sticky!"

They ran to Miss Cavendish's cabinet. Eddie ducked behind his squirrel and didn't see the rest. But he could still hear their voices.

"What does it say?"

"I can't see."

"Let *me* look. I can read it. It says 'the library.'"

"What does *that* mean?"

"You have to put the words together. From *all* the stickies."

"Yeah, right. Hey, I get it! 'Please . . . save . . . the library.'"

"Really?"

"Sure! Ms. Grisch still has the first two stickies on her computer. If you read them together, they say, 'Please save the library.'"

"But how did a sticky get way up there?"

There was a pause.

"Do you think . . . "

A long silence followed. Eddie squirmed.

"Miss Cavendish! Wow! For sure."

"You think so?"

"Yeah! Ghosts can go anywhere."

"So *that's* what Miss Cavendish wants us to save? The library?"

"Yeah. She's sending us a message!"

Eddie smiled. From what he knew of Miss Cavendish, he was sure she *would* want to save the Library, if she could.

The bell rang then. From his hiding spot behind

the squirrel, Eddie watched the children hurry out. As the Announcements began, he settled down to wait.

When the Library door opened again, it went *KA-BANG!*

The Grischer was back, and with her, the Principal.

"Look!" she said, pulling him to Miss Cavendish's cabinet. "Up there! Another one of those wretched stickies! When I came in here earlier, it was *moving.* It was slithering up the cabinet. It *talked* to me."

"Excuse me?" said the Principal. "Who . . . er . . . what talked to you?"

"That *sticky*! That yellow one. Up there."

Behind the wooden squirrel, Eddie twitched in surprise.

"It spoke?" said the Principal. "And . . . um . . . what did it say?"

"Well, how would I know?" said the Grischer. "It had a very quiet voice."

"The sticky," repeated the Principal.

"Yes! Of course. The sticky! I couldn't make out what it said. But it spoke just as surely as I'm speaking to you now. Don't you *see*, Mr. Steadman? It's part of the haunting!"

"The . . . er . . . what? Haunting? Oh, heavens, are you talking about the Miss Cavendish story?"

"Well, of course," said the Grischer. "I'm talking about the old lady who died. Right here! In that very rocking chair—the chair that *tripped* me when I first arrived. And excuse me, this is not a laughing matter."

"Oh, Ms. Grisch," said the Principal, trying to control his chuckles. "Poor Miss Cavendish died more than twenty years ago. What do you expect me to do?"

"I expect you to stop wasting time," said the Grischer. "Call the police, call a minister, call a medium! Just . . . solve the problem."

The Principal sighed.

"Look," he said. "I am removing the sticky from the little books. Hello, sticky? Anyone home? It's not speaking now, Ms. Grisch, you are safe. Do you still have the other stickies?"

"Yes, of course," said the Grischer. "I stuck them to my computer. Come with me."

Peeking out, Eddie saw the Grischer pulling the Principal along by his sleeve.

"Here!" she said when they reached the Librarian's desk. "Evidence!"

The Principal stared at the two stickies stuck to the computer screen. He added the new one. Now there were three in a row.

"Please . . . save . . . the library," read the Principal. "Hmm. Interesting writing, don't you think?"

"Not made by a *human* hand," said the Grischer.

She's got that right, thought Eddie.

"What I'm wondering," said the Principal, "is where these stickies came from." He glanced around the tidy desk. Then he grabbed the handle on the drawer and jiggled it.

"Oh, that!" muttered the Grischer. "It's stuck. Useless!"

"Hmm," said the Principal. "Let's give it a try."

He pulled on the drawer. It didn't move. He pulled harder, bracing himself with his other arm. The drawer opened slowly, with a squawk of protest.

On top of the cabinet, Eddie stopped breathing. Aunt Min!

Fortunately, the drawer wouldn't open all the way. Only far enough for the Principal to find the blank pad of stickies.

"Look!" he said, holding it up.

"Let me see," demanded the Grischer, seizing the pad.

"And what's this?" The Principal had something tiny on his fingertip. He held it up to the light. Then he held it to his nose.

"Interesting," he said. "Licorice."

"Disgusting." The Grischer looked closer. Then she let out a cry.

"It's been chewed!" she said. "Someone has deliberately left *a chewed-up lump of licorice* in my desk."

The Principal patted her shoulder. "I'm sure there's a sensible explanation. Why don't I speak to Mr. Iversen about it? Ask him to clean the drawer out. See if he can fix it."

As he spoke, he tried to shove the drawer closed again. When that didn't work, he leaned over. Then—*WHAM!*—the Principal threw his whole considerable weight against the drawer, shoulder first.

Eddie went rigid. He hoped he was wrong. He hoped the new thought in his head was completely and utterly wrong.

"There we go," said the Principal, rubbing his shoulder. "Now why don't you come along to the teachers' room, Ms. Grisch? We'll make some chamomile tea . . . and perhaps you can have a little lie-down?"

The Grischer rose to her full imposing height. "A lie-down? I have a class arriving in three minutes, Mr. Steadman. Why don't *you* lie down? Better still, find out who's been *spitting* in my desk."

She snatched up a tissue and used it to pick up the licorice lump, which the Principal had placed on her desk. "Evidence!" she snapped, holding it in the air. "I shall keep it right here until action is taken. I shall keep the stickies, too!"

The Principal stared for a moment at the licorice, being brandished now like a trophy. He let out a sigh.

"As you wish," he said, and left.

Up on the cabinet, Eddie barely listened, so badly did he long to run back to his aunt. Alas, it was impossible. For the rest of the morning, the Grischer never once left the Library. Classes came. Classes went. Children clustered in small groups, whispering and nudging one another. And as much as the Grischer tried to discourage it, nearly all of the children ended up, at some point, lingering beside the librarian's desk long enough to read the three yellow stickies lined up on her computer.

"Move along now," ordered the Grischer. "Get away from here, all of you. Why are you loitering?

Don't you know that curiosity killed the cat?"

"Cat?" said a child with a high, squeaky voice. "Is there . . . a *cat* ghost, too?"

"Cool!" said someone else.

Through all of this, Eddie remained trapped behind the squirrel, utterly distraught. He couldn't think of anything except the next bell. *When* would it ring? When would they *leave*?

The instant the room emptied, he ran! He raced across the cabinet, then slid, dangerously fast, down its side. Hitting the floor with a thud, he staggered, then ran again for the desk. He heard his own voice, frantic, in his head. "Aunt Min! Aunt Min!"

The drawer, when he got there, was shut tight. Firm and flat. Not even the thinnest, tiniest opening remained.

No way to get in.

No way to get out.

CHAPTER
22

As slowly as a snail and very carefully, Eddie crawled back and forth across the front of the drawer, searching for a way in.

There was a keyhole. Alas, it was tiny. Too small for even a bug to get through. But at least he could speak into it. He peered into the dark interior of the drawer.

"Aunt Min? It's me, Eddie! Are you there?"

He held his breath. Horrible images formed in his mind. Aunt Min suffocating for lack of oxygen. Aunt Min crushed at the back of the drawer.

"Eddie?" she said.

"Oh, good," he blurted. "Are you all right?"

"Yes, dear, as fine as possible under the circum—"

"HI, Eddie," said a second voice.

"Huh?" said Eddie. "Who's that?"

"It's Alfie," said Min.

"Alfie! What's *he* doing here?"

Alfie answered for himself, his voice echoing. "I came to SAVE YOU, Eddie. You've been gone ALL WEEK. Ma and Pa are going BUGGY."

"What?" Eddie struggled to absorb this. "Did you tell them where I went?"

"No," said Alfie. "If I did, they'd come AFTER YOU. They'd come AFTER ME, TOO. And they'd be MAD!"

Eddie was still confused. "Well . . . how did you get in *there*?"

Min's voice was impatient. "How do you *think* he got in? He showed up during Announcements. He was wandering around, hollering your name. Louder than a cricket at sundown! I made him hide in here to be—"

"SAFE!" said Alfie. "She said I'd be SAFE here. And now I'm not safe at ALL. Now I'm in PRISON!" Alfie let out a wail, a kind of high *KRRREEEEEEE* sound that was so piercing, it could be heard even by a Squisher.

"Alfie, hush!" said Min in such a stern voice, he obeyed.

Eddie clung to the keyhole in misery. "It's all my fault, Aunt Min."

"YES, IT IS!" yelled Alfie. *"KRRREEEEEE!"*

"Listen, Eddie—" began Min.

"I'm the one who put you in the drawer," interrupted Eddie. *"I'm* the one who wrote the stickies and scared the Grischer and made the Principal come and got you locked in that desk—"

"And ME, TOO!" yelled Alfie. "I'm LOCKED in here, too. Me and Auntie Min are stuck in here

FOREVER, Eddie, for the rest of our LIVES, and it's ALL YOUR FAULT! *KRREEEEEEEE!*"

"Oh, for heaven's sake!" said Min. "Cut it out, both of you. Eddie, this is *not* your fault. You've been nothing but brave and helpful. If it weren't for you, I'd be finished—as dead as poor Miss Cavendish. You have saved my life every single day, and that's the truth."

Eddie didn't have tear ducts, so he couldn't cry. But he sure *felt* like crying. "Really?"

"Really."

"But . . . what do we do?"

There was a long silence.

"I don't know, dear. I'm not going to lie—we're in a jam. I don't worry for myself. But I'm *very* sorry this is the day Alfie happened to—"

"KREEEEEEEEEEEEE!"

"Stop it, Alfie! I'm *sorry* that Alfie is trapped. If it's anyone's fault, it's mine. Your parents will never forgive me, and they're right."

"Oh, Aunt Min . . ."

"Eddie, listen, you can't stay here. It's Friday

lunch. The book club will be meeting any moment. You need to hide. We'll talk later."

Eddie knew this made sense. But it nearly broke his heart to crawl away from that keyhole, leaving his brother and his aunt trapped in—Alfie was right—a jail.

There was nowhere to go but the floor. All afternoon, he huddled against a desk leg, overwhelmed by sad thoughts. Somehow he had managed to fail at everything. He was supposed to rescue his aunt, and he hadn't. He was supposed to save the Library, and he hadn't. He was supposed to prove to his parents that he wasn't a nincompoop. . . and he *certainly* hadn't done that!

Instead, his aunt and his brother were now trapped in a space that could easily become their grave.

When the school day ended, the Grischer brought in more cardboard boxes. She began filling them with books, muttering unhappily the whole time.

"Hogwash!" she said as she slammed books into the box. "Drivel! What a useless pile of hooey!"

Her phone rang, and she slipped into her chair.

"Yes, Robert," she said to her brother. "I'm working on it right now. Dumping the magic books. Harry Potter, blah-blah-blah. The last thing this library needs is flying wizards. Bad enough that it has this weird . . . *presence*. Honestly, I can feel it. This very second."

Eddie flinched. Presence? Was she talking about him?

"I notice," added the Grischer, "that it hovers . . . right around this desk. Yes. Definitely! There's something about this hideous old desk."

Uh-oh, thought Eddie.

When she hung up the phone, she didn't go back to packing. Instead, she sat stiffly in her chair, her black-booted feet still as death. She stayed there for a strangely long time. Not moving. What was she doing?

And then Eddie knew. *She was listening.*

Alarmed, he listened too. Could Min accomplish a miracle? Could she keep his brother quiet in the drawer?

At last, the Grischer stood up. Eddie listened for the *tink* of the hanger as she put on her coat. He waited for the *click* that announced the locking of the Library door.

Then he crawled up to the keyhole.

"Aunt Min?"

"Eddie?"

"I won't leave you, I promise. I'm not going anywhere. I'm going to stay right here and make sure you have food and—"

"Eddie, stop," said Aunt Min. "You have to go home. Let me tell you why. Your parents are frantic right now. They've lost you, they've lost Alfie, and they don't know what's going on. I know it's hard, but you have to go back and tell them. We'll be okay here. It's Friday, so the school will be closed for two days. We'll be fine."

"But Aunt Min, you need food."

"Yes, we do. Before you go, you can fetch some. Do you think you'll be able to push it through this keyhole?"

"Oh, yes," said Eddie. It was such a small thing to do.

"Thank you," said Min.

"I'll be right back. Stay where you are."

Realizing what he had said, Eddie clapped a foot over his mouth.

Aunt Min managed a weak laugh. "We'll stay here, Eddie. No problem."

"*KRRRREEEEEEEEEEEEEE!*" wailed Alfie.

CHAPTER
23

In the end, Eddie didn't go home till Sunday. It took that long to fetch enough food for Aunt Min and Alfie. He raided the teachers' room again and again, relieved each time to see no further sign of the Mouse.

Min thought he was bringing too much food.

"Really, Eddie," she protested as he pushed more bread crumbs through the keyhole, "we already have a big stash."

"Can you get some more LICORICE?" asked Alfie. "The SQUISHERS took it AWAY!"

"Alfie, hush," said Min.

Eddie just kept gathering more food, not daring to name his worst fear. What if something happened to him on the way home? What if he got hurt or squished? And couldn't come back? And never got a chance to tell his parents? Dying of squishing would be bad. But dying of slow starvation in a drawer would be horrific. He couldn't leave till Min and Alfie had as much food as possible.

Aunt Min may have been thinking the same thing. She waited till Sunday morning to say, in her firmest voice, "Go home, Eddie. Now! Eyes open, antennae up. No dawdling, no daydreaming. And Eddie?"

"Yes?"

"Tell your parents I'm sorry. Tell them. . . ." Her voice faltered.

"I will."

It was good that the school was empty. Even so, Eddie had to be careful. You never could tell about a school on the weekend. There could be science fairs. Band practices. Sports games. Meetings. There was no way to know.

The first part of the journey was easy. Morning

sun poured through the big front door of Ferny Creek Elementary, its beams bright with dust motes, dancing above Eddie's head. Eddie stared up, entranced, at a secret universe he had never noticed before. He thought of *Horton Hears a Who!* Were there tiny creatures up there, living on those specks of dust? Did the creatures have families? Nephews? Aunties? Brothers?

"'A person's a person, no matter how small,'" said Eddie out loud.

He turned toward home. Before him stretched the great hallway, and again, he felt awed by its vastness. He began to walk.

He was nearing the halfway point when he spotted a dark blur. Looking more closely, he made out . . . legs. Lots of them.

Oh, no, thought Eddie. Not *you* again.

But there it was—the Spider. That very same stalker he had met before, so tall and fierce. Crouched now against the baseboard, it stood right in Eddie's path, waiting.

This time, there was no boy.

If Eddie tried to walk past, it would block his path. He knew it. It would force him back.

He *couldn't* go back.

Suddenly he remembered the Mouse. Eddie had *faced* the Mouse! He had faced that Mouse and survived.

Standing taller now, he faced the Spider.

It didn't move.

Was this some kind of trap?

Creeping forward, almost into striking range, Eddie began to sense that the spider's stillness was not what he had thought. The closer he got, the more certain he grew—

The Spider was dead.

It had somehow just *died* on its way down the hall.

This should have made Eddie feel better. But as he looked into the Spider's strange eyes, he found himself wondering, as he had already wondered about the dead fly and the dust creatures—did the Spider have a family?

He thought about his *own* family. He had never been away from them for so long. He hurried on. It was midday when he arrived at Room 19. He paused in the doorway to look for his raisin. Gone.

At that moment, the smells of the room—*his* very own classroom—washed over him. The chalk, the felt markers, the apple cores. The cough drops Mr. Patullo kept in his desk. Frankie the

guinea pig, who had visited the class in March—
only for two weeks, but his smell lingered on.

Home!

A surge of excitement rushed through him. He
ran toward the chalkboard, eager to see Ma and
Pa and tell them all about—

He stopped.

Remembered. Aunt Min, Alfie.

His feet dragged as he walked the final steps.
It was like walking through carpet.

CHAPTER
24

"EDDIE! EDDIE! EDDIE!"

The second Eddie stepped into the crack in the wall, he was swarmed. Everyone wanted a hug. With so many sisters and brothers, Eddie was all but trampled in the rush.

When he finally broke free, Ma and Pa were waiting.

"Sweetheart, darling, Eddie!" Ma clutched him to her thorax. Pa clasped them both, creating such a tangled knot that they all toppled over.

"He's home!" cried Pa, as he hauled himself to his feet. "Our boy is really home."

Eddie tried to enjoy the moment. It wouldn't last.

"Eddie?" Ma looked past him. "Have you seen Alfie? He disappeared two days ago. We thought he might have gone after you. Oh, Pa, where could he be?"

"Ma, wait," said Eddie. "I know where Alfie is. He *did* follow me—to the Library. He's there now, with Aunt Min."

"Thank goodness!" Ma sagged with relief. "But why didn't they come home?"

Eddie took a very deep breath. Then he told his parents everything—not hiding any of his own mistakes, not trying to blame anyone but himself. Not even the Grischer.

When he finished, no one spoke. Everyone—

his parents, his little brothers and sisters, his *very* little brothers and sisters—just stood there, staring at him with blank expressions. They seemed to be waiting for a happy ending.

"I'm sorry," said Eddie. "I'm

so very, very sorry."

"I don't understand," said Pa. "Is there no way at *all* to get that drawer open?"

Eddie shook his head.

"And there's no other way out?"

Eddie crumpled with misery. "The keyhole's too narrow."

"No way . . . at all?" whispered Ma.

"No."

A gloom descended. Nobody blamed Eddie. There were no why-didn't-you's or you-should-have's or if-only's. There was nothing but an enormous sense of loss. Ma and Pa slumped against one another, too wretched to move. The crack-in-the-wall was more crowded than ever, but Eddie could feel the cold, empty spaces that *should* have been filled by Alfie and Min. He would have done anything to bring them home.

Sitting there with his grieving family, who just a moment before had been so happy, Eddie felt a pain so fierce, it was like being squished—like having a giant foot come down and flatten him to a paste.

He stood it as long as he could. Then he rose firmly onto all six feet.

"Ma? Pa? I'm going back."

"What?" Ma stirred from her grief. "You certainly are not."

"Yes, I am. It's my fault they're trapped there, and I'll get them out—even if I have to eat a hole through that desk."

"Don't be ridiculous," said Ma. "Pa! He thinks he's a *termite* now. He thinks—"

"Let him go," said Pa. "He's right. They need looking after."

"What?" said Ma. "You mean . . . forever?"

Eddie nodded. "If necessary. I'll stay as long as I have to."

"Let him go," said Pa. "I'd do it myself if my legs were up to it, but—"

"They aren't," said Eddie. "It has to be me."

And that's how, half an hour later, he found himself hiking past the dead spider again. His parents had agreed that he should return to the Library as quickly as possible. The Squishers would be back in the morning

He reached the Library just before sundown. Shadows filled the corners. Silence filled the room. Even the clouds through the skylight looked gloomy.

"Aunt Min? Alfie?" he called, when he reached the keyhole.

"Eddie?" Alfie's voice was unusually quiet. "Is that you?"

"Yeah, it's me. You okay?"

"I guess," said Alfie. "Auntie Min's not so good."

"What do you mean?"

"Well, she's . . . sad."

"Oh," said Eddie. "Where is she? In the secret compartment?"

"Yeah. She's not moving much."

"Oh," said Eddie again. "Do you have enough food?"

"Lots," said Alfie. "We're not very hungry. Do you want me to push some out for you?"

"Okay." Eddie waited as Alfie forced a bit of apple through the keyhole. "Thanks."

And there Eddie stayed, clinging to the keyhole for as long as he could, nibbling on apple and trying to cheer up his little brother. When he could hang on no longer, he climbed up on top of the desk. That's where he spent the night. Out in the open. Alone.

He had lots of time to think. And worry.

Yes, he could feed Min and Alfie. He could keep them from starving. But how long would that last? How long before the Grischer, eager to transform the Library, decided to dump the old desk, along with its tiny inhabitants?

Did Aunt Min know how much the Grischer hated the desk? Did she understand how bad the situation was?

Yes, of course she did. That's why she was sad.

As the sun rose, Eddie crawled underneath the desk. He tucked himself up next to the wooden leg. This would be his new home. This floor. This dust.

Suddenly he wished, with all his heart that he too had gotten trapped in the desk drawer.

CHAPTER
25

The first thing Eddie saw when he woke up
Monday morning was the Grischer's feet. Again,
he had missed her arrival. And now as he roused
himself, there they were, right in his face—two
long, narrow feet wearing pointy suede boots the
color of a fawn.

It was not a good start to the day.

A moment later, the Library door opened.
KA-BANG!

"Can we come in, Ms. Grisch?"

Eddie perked up. It was Hazel! Other children
giggled in the background.

"We just want to peek," said Hazel.

"Peek?" said the Grischer. "Peek at what?"

"At the bookshelves," said Hazel. "We want to see if there are any new stickies."

"I've already checked," said the Grischer, "and—wait a minute! What's that you're wearing on your shirt?"

Hazel stepped forward while her friends scattered to the shelves. Eddie watched their feet rush past.

"Do you mean this?" said Hazel. "It's a button. See? The kind you pin on. My mom has a machine to make them. For her store in the mall. It's called Whoopsidoodle, and it has—"

"Never mind what it has. Show me the button."

"Sure," said Hazel. "See? It says 'please save the library.' Just like the stickies!" Her voice bubbled with excitement. "We made twenty-five on Saturday. Yellow like the stickies."

There was a silence. The Grischer's long legs twisted slowly around one another. "Are other students wearing these buttons, too?"

"Yeah, lots," said Hazel. "But we haven't given them all away yet. Would you like one?"

"No!" said the Grischer abruptly. "But—"

"It's okay," said Hazel. "We can make more."

At that moment, a pair of red shoes came bounding into view—one of Hazel's friends. "No new stickies this morning!" reported Marigold from Room 19.

"We looked all over," added Lucy, right behind.

"That's okay," said Hazel. "We can't expect a new sticky every day. Bye, Ms. Grisch. See you later!"

As the girls left, they passed two more children coming in. Boys, from the look of their shoes— brown sandals and black-and-white high-tops. They were pulling a grown-up Squisher—men's loafers.

"Just came to take a look at the rocking chair," said the Squisher. "I remember the old days when Miss Cavendish used to visit. My boys are all excited that I knew her. Hey, yeah, there it is. The chair! Wow! Look at it."

"Yes," said the Grischer sourly. "*Look* at it."

"Want to see my new button, Ms. Grisch?" said one of the boys. "It looks just like the yellow stickies."

"Mine, too," said the other. "See?"

"Great idea, these buttons," said the big Squisher. "I've been trying to get my boys to read more. Maybe you have some suggestions?"

The Grischer was obliged to follow them to the bookshelves.

Watching from under the desk, Eddie was dumbfounded. He had listened—to Hazel, to the boys and their father—with growing astonishment. Buttons? His stickies had been turned into *buttons*? And the children were wearing them at school? How amazing was that?

Not as amazing, it turned out, as what happened next . . .

THUMP went the floor behind Eddie.

"YOW!" said a familiar voice.

Eddie turned. "Alfie?"

Alfie lay flipped on his back on the linoleum floor, his legs waving wildly. After an awkward roll, he clambered to his feet.

"Alfie!" whispered Eddie, rushing over. "How did you get here?"

"I FELL!" said Alfie. "It really HURT, Eddie!"

"Shh!" Eddie listened for the Grischer's voice.
It was faint now, in the distance. "Okay, tell me,
quick—how did you get out of the drawer?"

"There's a little GAP at the back." Alfie danced
in excited circles. "Between the DRAWER and
the TOP of the DESK. I FOUND it, Eddie, all by
MYSELF! Auntie Min didn't even know it was
there. YOU didn't know about it, either."

"Wow, Alfie, that's great! We can get Aunt Min
out, too."

Alfie stopped dancing. "Uh, no. We can't."

"Why not?"

"I had to FALL, Eddie. There's nothing to hold ONTO. I just FELL!"

Eddie sighed. Alfie was right. Min couldn't handle a long drop onto a hard floor.

"Anyway, she's too BIG," said Alfie. "It's a WEENSY gap. I had to SQUISH to get through."

"Oh, Alfie, don't say *squish*."

"I know," said Alfie. "Auntie Min didn't like it, either. But I only squished MYSELF, Eddie. I HAD to. And I'm OKAY, see?" He did another prance.

"Keep your voice down, Alfie, I mean it." Quickly, Eddie explained about the Grischer— her exceptional hearing, her stealthy prowling, her speed and skill with a magazine.

"Yeah, I KNOW all that. Auntie Min TOLD me."

"Is Aunt Min okay?"

Alfie shuffled his feet. "Not really. She hardly moves, and she won't eat. But she was glad I found that GAP, Eddie. She TOLD me to go. It was HER idea."

Eddie nodded, not surprised.

Alfie looked around.

"WOW!" he said. "Look at all this SPACE!" He ran in a big circle under the desk. Then dashed right into the open.

"HEY!" yelled Eddie. "Get back here!"

Alfie took far too much time to obey. On his way back, he spotted the shriveled remains of the blueberry behind a cord. He beetled over and poked them with his foot. "Can we EAT this?"

Without waiting for an answer, he raced to the pad of stickies and crawled on top. "Is this where you SLEEP? What're we going to do NOW? PLAY? I've been ALL COOPED UP, Eddie. Let's DO something!"

It was time, Eddie decided, to set his little brother straight.

"Alfie," he said in a quiet voice that he hoped would be an example, "there are three important rules here. Rule number one—keep quiet. Rule number two—keep quiet. Rule number three—"

"KEEP QUIET?"

"Right. And I know you're not good at rules. . . ." He thought for a moment. Alfie was *terrible* at rules. "What did Aunt Min say to keep you quiet?"

"Oh." Alfie looked uncomfortable. "She said . . . well, she said that if I didn't shut up, she'd EAT ME. I think she MEANT it, Eddie."

"Oh," said Eddie. "Well then . . . that goes double for me, Alfie. If you don't keep quiet, I will . . . er . . . eat you!"

He gave Alfie his fiercest, hungriest stare, hoping the threat would work. It seemed unlikely. Who'd want to eat *Alfie*?

He was surprised to see his brother twitch nervously. "Okay. I'll be quiet."

"Good," said Eddie. "Excellent."

What Eddie *didn't* say was how glad he was to have company again—even if it was just Alfie. There's nothing like being alone for a few days, with no one to talk to and nothing to look at except shoes, to make you appreciate your little brother, however annoying he might be.

And so the brothers spent the day together, listening as the children came and went.

One thing they discovered quickly—Hazel's buttons were a great success. In each visiting class, there were children proudly wearing "please save the library" buttons, and many more children who wanted one.

There was chatter about the Library Ghost, too. The Grischer tried to stop it, but she couldn't be everywhere at once. So over the course of the day, listening to the children, Eddie and Alfie managed to piece together an interesting story.

They found out that some of Ferny Creek's students, including Hazel, had had a busy weekend. The mysterious yellow stickies that had appeared in the Library the week before had aroused the children's curiosity, especially about the Library Ghost. They had become so curious about Miss Cavendish, in fact, that they'd searched for people who had known her. There were plenty of those around—parents, grandparents, neighbors. The children had asked lots of questions.

And on Monday in the Library, those same children told Eddie and Alfie—without meaning to, of course, and without even knowing the bugs were *there*—what they had learned about Miss Cavendish.

Like the fact that she was famous for her cookies. She called them Cavendish Cookies and always arrived with a jar full, asking the children to help her out because "I made too many." She liked birthdays, too—anybody's, everybody's— and thought books were the best gift of all. Also, she really did have a dog—a golden retriever named Charlotte Brontë who loved, more than anything, to be read to. Dogs were not allowed in Ferny Creek Elementary, but an exception was made for Charlotte Brontë because so many children had learned to read by having her as their audience.

And then there was the whoopee cushion. Miss Cavendish's nephew gave it to her for her birthday, and she liked to bring it to school and hide it on the comfy couch or the story-time chair. After it made its noise, she would put it away again till everyone forgot about it. She brought it out only once or twice a year, but there were plenty of adults in Ferndale who still remembered Whoopee Cushion Day.

"What's a WHOOPEE CUSHION?" asked Alfie.

"Shh," said Eddie.

The bugs also learned that occasionally Miss Cavendish would read to herself in some corner of the Library and entirely forget where she was. Children would give a gentle poke to rouse her. She called it her "reading trance."

Eddie grinned when he heard this. That was exactly what happened to him—a reading trance. He just hadn't known what to call it.

Eddie loved the stories about the Library Ghost, but the whole time he was listening, all he could think about was Aunt Min.

Could she hear the stories? Eddie hoped so.

And when the stranger came into the Library

at the end of the day, Eddie hoped that Aunt Min could hear *her* too.

The stranger was a complete surprise.

Her name was Adelaide Glossup, and she knew more about the Library Ghost than anyone else in Ferndale.

CHAPTER
26

When Adelaide Glossup stepped into the Library, she clapped both hands to her cheeks. "Aunt Louisa's cabinet! I haven't seen that in years!"

Without another word, she walked straight to Miss Cavendish's brightly painted cabinet. The Principal followed, while under the desk, Eddie and Alfie settled down to watch.

"My aunt Louisa made furniture," said Adelaide Glossup, running her hand over the woodwork. "She was quite well known, and this is an especially beautiful piece. Oh, look! Some of Aunt Lou's old books are still on the shelves."

She reached for one. "I don't believe it! Here's *Anne of Green Gables*. My favorite book as a child . . . and this was the very copy I read."

"A classic," said the Principal, smiling agreeably. "And so is this cabinet. So kind of your aunt to donate it to our Library."

"Excuse me?" said a quiet voice.

The Principal jumped. "Oh! Ms. Grisch! I didn't notice you there. This is Adelaide

Glossup. She's the niece of our famous Miss Cavendish."

"I see," said the Grischer. But it was clear from her voice that she didn't see at all.

Adelaide Glossup pointed at the cabinet. "I wanted to see *this* again. One of your students—a little girl named Hazel—is my neighbor. She came to see me on Saturday, asking about my aunt. What a surprise! I thought everyone had forgotten Aunt Lou by now."

"Oh, she's not forgotten here," said the Principal, smiling.

"I can see that. There's one of her rocking chairs, too. She made three or four of those. Called them her Reading Rockers. I can't tell you what a pleasure it is, Mr. Steadman, to see Aunt Lou's work here. I know how she loved this Library."

Eddie and Alfie listened to all this from a distance, of course. But closer to the cabinet, some fifth graders were researching weather and climate.

One of them, a girl, spoke up now. "There's a picture of Miss Cavendish *here*, Mr. Steadman. In our Library."

"There is?" said the Principal. "Where, Tanika?"

"Over by the atlases. I'll show you."

A moment later, the Principal was back, blowing dust off a framed photograph. "Tanika's right. I have no idea how this photo got hidden away back there. We must bring it into the open." He propped it against some books on the cabinet.

"Are you sure that's wise?" asked the Grischer. "Ms. Glossup, you may not be aware, but there have been some very disturbing *manifestations* in this room. Sounds. Sightings. Messages. Mr. Steadman is aware of the details."

"Oh, yes," said Adelaide Glossup. "Hazel told me. My aunt seems to have become a bit of a . . . legend in this Library."

"Exactly," said the Principal. "*Legend*. Not ghost."

Ms. Glossup chuckled. "Well, I don't believe in ghosts, and neither did Aunt Lou. But I love the idea that her spirit lives on in this Library. She was a remarkable woman. Had a huge influence on all of us—her nieces and nephews. Most of all on my cousin Gregory, of course."

"Gregory?" repeated the Principal. "Cavendish? Excuse me? Do you mean . . . Gregory Cavendish? The writer?"

"Why, yes. He's my cousin."

"Gregory Cav—I just read his new book. Didn't he win—"

"Yes," said Ms. Glossup.

"Oh, my goodness!" The Principal was suddenly breathless. "I had heard that Gregory Cavendish had some connection to Ferndale, but I never imagined he had anything to do with . . . my goodness, this is amazing!"

"Aunt Lou encouraged Greg," said Ms. Glossup. "His reading, of course. Then his writing. He talks about her often."

"My goodness!" said the Principal for the third time.

"Yes, indeed," said Adelaide Glossup with a

smile. "Well, thank you, Mr. Steadman, it's been a real pleasure to visit. So many wonderful memories of Aunt Lou." She returned *Anne* to the cabinet.

"Not at all." The Principal beamed. "Come anytime."

In a rush of good feelings, the Principal and Ms. Glossup left the Library. The fifth graders left soon after.

But three of them stayed behind. Two boys and a girl.

"Ms. Grisch?" said one of the boys.

"That's Janek," whispered Eddie to his brother.

"Who's Janek?" asked Alfie.

"Aren't you . . . the young man who helped me pack boxes?" asked the Grischer.

"Yes," said Janek. "And I . . . I mean we . . . were wondering. Can we please unpack the graphic novels?"

"Excuse me?" said the Grischer. *"Unpack?"*

"Yes," said the other boy. "We're writing our own graphic novels. Me, Janek, and Emma. For our social studies projects. Janek told us you put the graphic novels in boxes. But we need them— for research."

"Plus we want to *be* graphic novelists," said the girl. "When we grow up."

"Not me," said Janek. "I want to be a cartoonist. In the *New Yorker*."

"I want to make books like Wimpy Kid," said the other boy.

"So you see," said the girl, "we need the books. Could we please unpack them, Ms. Grisch?"

"For heaven's sake," said the Grischer. "Can't you get them out of the *public* library?"

All three children stared at her in shock.

"Oh, very well," said the Grischer. "As if I don't have enough to do."

A few minutes later, Eddie and Alfie were treated to the odd sight—or at least it looked odd to Eddie—of the Grischer packing the science fiction books into boxes while the fifth graders *unpacked* the graphic novels out of other boxes.

"I don't UNDERSTAND the Squishers," said Alfie.

"Don't worry about it," said Eddie. "None of us do."

And with that, he felt a sudden pang. Out of all the bugs in the family, the one who had the best understanding of the peculiarities of Squishers was Aunt Min. She would definitely have something to say about these boxes.

How Eddie missed his aunt. And how he would have loved to set her free!

CHAPTER
27

The moment the Grischer left for the day, Eddie and Alfie scurried up the desk leg.

"Aunt Min?" said Eddie through the keyhole. "Are you there?"

"Hey, Auntie!" said Alfie. "Look at ME! I'm OUT of PRISON! I'm FREEEEE!"

"Alfie, stop it," said Eddie.

It took a long time for Min to reach the keyhole.

"I'm so glad," she said hoarsely. "Alfie . . . free."

Eddie peeked inside. "Are you okay?"

She looked awful. He couldn't see much in the murkiness of the drawer, but he could tell she was wasting away.

"You have to eat more," he told her. "Alfie and I are going to the teachers' room tonight. We'll find you something tasty."

She didn't answer.

"Aunt Min?"

He couldn't tell whether she had walked away or just dropped to the bottom of the drawer. Either way, it wasn't good.

"Aunt Min? Are you okay?"

In the teachers' room later that night, Eddie and Alfie found a chunk of pear, only slightly spoiled, as well as a cracker and a jelly bean. Eddie told Alfie to leave the jelly bean behind.

"It's not food, Alfie."

"So what?" said Alfie. "YOU got to eat LICORICE! Auntie Min even said so. You got to eat it ALL NIGHT LONG!"

"What?" said Eddie.

"And you ate it ALL UP! You didn't leave any for ME!" added Alfie. "Only a horrible LUMP full of SPIT!"

Eddie reeled backward. He was so mad, he started yelling the same way his brother did. "What are you TALKING about, Alfie? I didn't WANT the licorice. I didn't even LIKE the licorice. I just—I just—oh for CRYING OUT LOUD, Alfie, go ahead and EAT THE JELLY BEAN!"

"Goody," said Alfie. "Thanks, Eddie."

Alfie ate a very big hole into the jelly bean. Then he gave a loud burp and was happy to leave the rest behind.

On the way back, both brothers carried chunks of pear for Min. She liked pear, Eddie knew, and it was full of water.

She probably needed water.

* * *

The Library was bathed in moonlight when they returned.

"Aunt Min?" called Eddie. "Are you there?"

"AUNTIE MIN! COME TO THE KEYHOLE!" hollered Alfie.

When she finally arrived, all she said was, "I'm not hungry."

"But you must be thirsty," said Eddie. "Eat this pear. Please. You need to keep your strength up so . . . so you can walk home, when we get you out."

Aunt Min managed, with great effort, to haul herself to the keyhole. Her eyes looked faded and dull.

"Oh," she croaked. "Moonlight . . . pretty."

Eddie couldn't speak.

"Eddie?" she whispered.

"Yes?"

"Don't get . . . hopes up."

"What do you mean?"

"I mean . . . glad Alfie's safe . . . but me . . . a good long life, Eddie . . . wonderful adventures . . . maybe I won't. . . ."

"Don't say it, Aunt Min!"

"Not the . . . worst thing . . . in the world."

"Yes, yes, it would be! It would be the worst thing ever! Don't give up. There must be *something* I can do."

"Sometimes," said Min slowly, "nothing . . . to do."

Impossible, thought Eddie.

That night he couldn't fall asleep. As his brother dozed on the pad of stickies under the desk, Eddie moved out into the open. He needed to gaze at the stars. He didn't believe in *wishing* on stars, but that night he felt desperate enough to try, choosing a particularly bright one that stood out from the others. It twinkled back in what seemed to be a friendly manner . . . but it offered no answer. Eddie wondered if his wish was too big.

Turning away, he searched his own brain instead. How could he rescue his aunt? Ideas came. None good. His mind raced in circles from one terrible idea to another. Round and round and round.

It was his worst night of worrying—ever.

CHAPTER
28

Tuesday began with a flurry of activity. Hazel's buttons had been noticed all through the school. Before classes even started, the Library was filled with children, parents, and teachers, all trying to find out more about the please-save-the-library campaign.

"Come ON," yelled Alfie. "Let's LISTEN!"

And before Eddie could stop him, he ran right out into the open, racing pell-mell along an electrical cord. Eddie gasped and dashed after him.

Seconds later they were both huddled behind a gray plastic box with cords plugged into it like the legs of an octopus. Alfie was quiet—a situation that might have had something to do with Eddie's deathly tight grip on his mandibles.

Together they listened to a group of adult Squishers. Parents, guessed Eddie.

"I don't get it," said a mother. "Save the library from what? Ms. Grisch, do you know?"

The Grischer cleared her throat. "Perhaps . . . excessive costs?"

"Costs?" said a father. "Of course there will be costs. Worth every cent, if you ask me. Just look at this space book. Amazing!"

The Grischer tried again. "But we have the internet now and . . ."

"The internet?" said someone else. "Hah! Ask the internet something, and you get 1000 answers, most of them useless. How are kids supposed to deal with that?"

"My kids *love* this library," said the father.

"Well, then, what are we saving it from?"

"I don't know," said the first mother. "But it's all Hazel talks about."

"It has something to do with Miss Cavendish,"

said a father who had just arrived. "Remember when we read to her dog?"

"Charlotte Brontë!" said the first mother.

Everyone laughed.

Alfie, meanwhile, was squirming madly. He had just noticed some children on the floor on the *other* side of the desk.

"COME ON!" he yelled, breaking free of Eddie's grip.

Fortunately the adult Squishers were far too busy to notice a small black bug running helter-skelter along the wall, followed closely by a larger and much greener bug.

Alfie charged underneath a book cart. Eddie was right on his tail. He dragged his little brother behind one of the cart's wheels. "That's IT! You STAY here!"

"Shh!" said Alfie. "They'll HEAR you!"

But the children, like the adults, were far too busy to notice the bugs. There were six of them, kneeling on the floor.

"What are you guys doing?" asked a new boy

who had just arrived.

"Making posters," said Hazel. "Marigold thought it up. Want to make one? Here, look at mine."

She held it so the boy could see. Eddie and Alfie could see, too. It had drawings of books and book characters around the edges. In the middle were large printed letters that said:

PLEASE

SAVE

THE

LIBRARY

Wesley, a boy Eddie knew from Room 19, spoke up. "Want to see mine?"

It said:

PLEASE

SAVE

THE

FERNY CREEK

LIBRARY

"Hey!" said Hazel. "Cool."

"Yeah," said Marigold. "Wesley's printing even looks like the stickies, too."

That was just the start. The hubbub went on all day. Posters, buttons, chatter. In the small world of Ferny Creek Elementary, the story of the little yellow stickies was becoming a very *big* deal. It spread through the school like mayflies on a warm spring evening. Nobody quite understood what was going on. (Well, of course not. How could they?) But everyone was intrigued.

The question on everyone's mind was the same: "Save the Library from what?"

That was the question the reporter from the *Ferndale Sentinel* asked when she visited the Library that afternoon.

"Save the Library from what?" she asked Ms. Grisch, pen and notebook in hand.

"Why are you asking *me*?" replied the Grischer. "Why don't you ask . . . the Principal?"

But the Principal, it seems, was busy elsewhere. He didn't turn up in the Library till late afternoon. And when he did, he was bouncing on his toes.

"Oh, Ms. Grisch," he said. "Isn't it wonderful? All this support, this interest in the Library?"

The Grischer didn't answer.

"Yes, well . . . ," said the Principal, "here's what I wanted to tell you. Some parents have been asking—quite a few parents actually, and they're meeting tonight—whether we might change the name of our Library. The teachers have asked the same thing. They all feel this is long overdue. So what do you think about changing the name of our Ferny Creek School Library to—"

He paused for effect. "The . . . Louisa . . . May . . . Cavendish . . . Memorial . . . Library!"

The Principal clapped gleefully, apparently hoping the Grischer would join in. "I spoke to Ms. Glossup, and it's possible—oh, my goodness!—that Gregory Cavendish himself will come for the ceremony. We'll go all out! Cookies, juice, balloons—the sky's the limit! A party, Ms. Grisch."

"YAAAAAY!" yelled Alfie.

"What?" said the Grischer. "WHAT? Did you hear that?"

"Hear what?" said the Principal.

"That squeaky sound?"

"What squeaky sound? Ms. Grisch, are you quite—"

"YAAAAAAAY!"

"There it is again! Just like last week. *The talking sticky!* I showed it to you, Mr. Steadman, last Friday. Didn't you hear that sound just now?"

"Er . . . no," said the Principal.

What happened next wasn't exactly clear to the bugs, but Mr. Steadman made the mistake of mentioning tea again.

"*Tea?*" said Grischer. "Again with the *tea*? Will you please stop offering me tea, Mr. Steadman! Just . . . just . . . just stop it!"

After the Principal left—he retreated very quickly—the Grischer phoned her brother.

"That's it," she told him. "I've had it! I am

leaving Ferny Creek, and I am *never* coming back."

Beneath the desk, Eddie was holding his brother in a four-footed headlock. There would be no more YAAAAYs from Alfie.

"No, Robert, I'm not saying there's a ghost here. I . . . well, to be honest . . . I don't *know* what it is. All I know is, there's something very peculiar in this Library that's been against us from the start."

There was a silence.

Then the Grischer stamped her foot. "No, it's not just a few kids and stickies! Why don't you come here and see for yourself? It's teachers. Parents. Reporters. It's the relatives of *dead volunteers*! Is that enough for you? Or shall I add Facebook and Twitter?"

Under the desk, Eddie decided to let Alfie go. He made a zipper motion across his mouth, signaling silence.

"Well, my advice is—drop the whole thing! Find something else to close. Ferny Creek Elementary

School is attached to its library like gum to a shoe. And by the way, Robert, I heard *your* name mentioned here today—and not in a good way. Watch your step."

This time when the Grischer left, the door slammed shut behind her, as if it was hastening her on her way. It slammed loud enough to make even a bug jump.

KA-BANG!

CHAPTER
29

The Grischer was gone.

It *should* have been a wonderful moment.

"Does this mean . . . you DID it?" Alfie was hopping like a flea. "WOO, WOO, Eddie, she's GONE! The Grischer's gone. YAAAAAY!"

Eddie knew he should be thrilled. He should be cheering with Alfie. But all he could think about, with the Library now safe, was the bug who had helped him save it.

"Let's go see Aunt Min," he said to his brother. "Right now. Come on, hurry!"

Filled with trepidation, they climbed the side of the desk.

"Hello?" said Eddie through the keyhole. "Are

you there, Aunt Min?"

He waited. "Hello?"

Alfie tried, too. "AUNTIE MIN?"

The silence that followed lasted way too long. A sick feeling rose in Eddie's belly. Why wasn't she answering?

"Is she okay?" whispered Alfie.

They took turns calling her. They called till they were hoarse.

No answer. All they could see through the keyhole was gloom. The only smell was rotting pear.

"We have to figure this out," muttered Eddie. "We *have* to get inside!"

For Alfie's sake, he kept his next thought private.

No matter what we find.

CHAPTER
30

When the door opened the next morning to the Ferny Creek Elementary School Library—soon to be known as the Louisa May Cavendish Memorial Library—a brand-new Squisher walked in.

KA-BANG!

Eddie and Alfie peeked around the desk leg.

The new Squisher was short and slim, and to Eddie's eyes, quite young. He had large, dark eyes and round glasses and a neat cap of short black hair. Eddie saw all this in a second, but the thing he really noticed was the man's vest. He wore it over a crisp white shirt, and the thing Eddie noticed was how *green* it was. The vest was a rich, shiny green.

KA-BANG!

The Principal burst through the door, breathing hard. "Thank you so much for coming, Mr. Banerjee. We've lost two librarians in the last week, and we're quite desperate."

The Squisher smiled. "I'm happy to help."

"Well then, here we are." The Principal gestured around. "The books, the carpet, the desk, and so on. Is it . . . all right?"

"All right?" said the Squisher. "Yes, it looks fine."

"Not too crowded? With . . . er, books?"

"Oh, no, not at all." The Squisher's voice was low and pleasant. "Plenty of room for *more* books, I'd say."

"Oh," said the Principal, glancing around. He stared at a half-empty shelf. "Well, that's odd. Er . . . do you have any . . . questions?"

But the Squisher was already taking himself on a tour. Pointing at the desk, he smiled. "Beautiful wood!"

He bent to touch the carpet. "Good and thick."

Sitting on the comfy couch, he bounced a couple of times. Then he patted the cushions. "I like bright colors in a library, don't you?"

Standing again, he wandered to the bookshelves. He bent to peer at the titles. He ran his hands over the spines.

"Some excellent new books here," he said, pulling one from the shelf. "Someone's taken a lot of care."

"Oh, yes," said the Principal. "That was our Ms. Laurel. She cared a great deal about books, and she wanted the very best."

"I can see that," said the Squisher. As he turned from the shelf, something caught his eye.

"Is that . . . Miss Cavendish's cabinet?" he asked.

"Oh, dear." The Principal wrung his hands. "How did you hear about *that*?"

"My wife," said the Squisher, smiling. "She went to school here. She knew Miss Cavendish. I've heard all the stories."

"You have?" The Principal's voice sounded strangled,

"Oh, yes. Even that last day in the Library when she . . . you know." The Squisher let his head drop slowly forward.

"Oh," said the Principal. "That. Yes."

A long pause followed.

The Principal took a deep breath. "You're not . . . I mean . . . well, that is to say . . . you're not afraid of ghosts, are you?"

The Squisher laughed. "Ghosts? Do you mean Miss Cavendish?" He laughed again. "I don't believe in ghosts, Mr. Steadman. But if Miss Cavendish ever comes calling in this Library, I will be tickled pink to meet her. And if she brings Charlotte Brontë, all the better."

"Charlotte—oh, you mean the dog?" The Principal chuckled happily. "Yes, of course. All wonderful nonsense, isn't it? I'm glad you're so sensible. Especially after—well, never mind that. I just want you to know that we're very happy to have you here, Mr. Banerjee. Welcome to Ferny Creek!"

He shook the Squisher's hand for an extra-long time. Then he left with a spring in his step.

"I LIKE the new Squisher," said Alfie.

"Let's wait and see," said Eddie. The Squisher *did* sound good. He liked the couch, he liked the books, he liked the Library Ghost.

But Eddie's thoughts were still on Aunt Min. It was hard to concentrate on anything else.

The first class to meet the new Squisher was second grade. They stared at him with curiosity as they sat on the story-time carpet. Eddie and Alfie watched from the desk leg.

"You can call me Mr. B if you like," said the Squisher.

B for books, thought Eddie.

A child raised a hand. "How long are you staying?"

"Good question," Eddie whispered to Alfie. "That's what I wanted to ask."

"I don't know," said the Squisher. "Right now I'm here for the day."

He held up a book. "Has anyone read this book? Do you recognize the cover?"

No one spoke.

The Squisher started to read. "'When Mr. Frederick C. Little's second son was born, everybody noticed that he was not much bigger than a mouse. . . .'"

Eddie jumped. His whole body sang. Was it possible? Out of all the books in the Library, Mr. B had chosen *Stuart Little*. It was like a sign! Suddenly Eddie knew with complete certainty who this Squisher was going to be. Mr. B wasn't just any ordinary Squisher. Mr. B was—

The New Librarian!

Alfie seemed to know it too. "Come ON!" he told Eddie. "Let's get CLOSER!"

And once again, Alfie did the unthinkable. Risking his life—and Eddie's, too—he charged right into the open.

"NOOO!" hollered Eddie. But it was too late. All he could do was dash after his brother, who had already reached the octopus-thing where all the wires met up. By the time Eddie got there, Alfie had run off again! Eddie finally caught up near the story-time chair. He tackled his brother and dragged him out of sight.

Thank goodness for *Stuart Little*! When Eddie looked around, he discovered to his enormous relief that nobody—not one single child—was looking at him or Alfie.

Everyone was looking at Mr. B.

And Mr. B was, of course, looking at *Stuart Little*.

So nobody saw Eddie and Alfie. But from their new position under a book rack, they now had a perfect close-up view of the children's faces. Here's what they saw. The children's eyes were wide, their chins were lifted, their mouths were slightly open. They were only doing what *any* Squisher does when listening to a story, of course. But Eddie had never seen it so clearly before.

He also noticed how the children were sitting. Some of them leaned against a friend or threw an arm over another child's shoulders. A boy at the edge flung his legs out straight and leaned back on his elbows. Noticing this, Alfie flung out his legs, too.

And Eddie? He leaned forward, listening to *Stuart* with every molecule in his body.

And as he listened, he forgot about being in the Library, about chasing a naughty brother, about having an aunt in a drawer. He forgot all his worries and problems. He even forgot about being a bug. For the time he was listening, Eddie was a mouse like Stuart Little, living with an ordinary family in a pleasant house in New York City.

The New Librarian's voice was warm and inviting. Even better, he could change it in an instant to the voices of the characters in the story—kids' voices, lady voices, and a very believable mouse voice for Stuart. Mr. B didn't just *read* the story. He *became* the story.

Aunt Min was right. This was magic.

CHAPTER
31

Maybe it was hearing *Stuart Little* that did it.

Or maybe it was the New Librarian with his kind brown eyes and his shiny green vest.

Or maybe it was the big, ripe blueberry that fell from a ziplock bag in the pocket of a kindergarten boy who arrived after recess in the Library. It bounced and rolled under the desk.

"WOW!" said Alfie.

One of these things—or maybe all three—made Eddie stand a bit straighter. It made him breathe more deeply and relax.

And *that's* when he got his idea for Aunt Min. It formed in his mind so suddenly, he felt almost dizzy.

Would it work? Would he have enough time? He wanted to try it now, right away. *Would it work?*

He was shaky with tension and hope.

As he gathered his tools, Alfie badgered him with questions. "Whatcha DOING, Eddie? What's GOING ON?"

No time to explain! Fortunately, Eddie had everything he needed, right there under the desk. He got to work.

Somewhere in the room he could hear the New Librarian talking to kindergarten about dinosaur feathers. Interesting as that was, Eddie blocked it out. Then he heard some kind of game, with the kindergarteners chanting and stomping. He ignored that, too. And finally there was Alfie, with his nonstop chatter. Eddie barely heard.

"Concentrate!" he told himself.

He worked harder and faster than he'd ever worked before. When lunchtime came, he was ready. The bell rang. The children bustled out to play. The New Librarian shelved books and left.

Eddie started his climb up the desk. This was the dangerous part.

KA-BANG!

He flinched at the sound. Someone was at the door. He could hear voices.

If anyone spotted Eddie—if anyone took a *good* look—it was all over.

Up he climbed as quickly as he could manage, not daring to look around or down or anywhere at all—

Until he reached the drawer.

"Hey, EDDIE!" said Alfie. "Can I HELP now? PLEEEASE!"

He had followed right behind. Brave Alfie! Together the two brothers finished the job.

Staring at the results, Eddie knew they had done everything they could. The rest was up to fate. They scooted back down and hid under the desk. Eddie crossed his antennae. Hoping . . .

Third grade was creating a play about pioneers. The New Librarian wandered among them, helping with research.

"Please," whispered Eddie. "Please come over here and look at the desk."

But Mr. B wandered away. Eddie tried to *will* him over.

"Heeeeere," he whispered. "Pleeeeeease."

Alfie whispered, too. "Heeeeere."

The minutes dragged past. Eddie paced restlessly back and forth beneath the desk. Finally he saw what he'd been longing to see— the New Librarian's gray-and-tan running shoes, coming his way. A pair of smaller shoes ran behind. Pink with curly laces.

"Let's see," said the New Librarian. "I'm sure there's some tape here somewhere."

Eddie tingled with anticipation.

"Hey!" said a girl's voice. "Look! A yellow sticky." Her curly-laced feet ran around the desk.

"Wow!" she said. "It's one of those stickies with the funny writing. It's stuck to the drawer. Is this Miss Cavendish again? Ooh!"

The New Librarian laughed. "It's only an

ordinary sticky. Let's have a look."

There were more shoes around the desk now as other children noticed what was happening.

"Hey!" said a voice. "Over here, everyone! Sophie found a new sticky."

More shoes. And more.

The chatter rose, along with the excitement. "Is it her?" asked the children. "Is it the ghost?"

"No ghost," said the New Librarian. "Just this little sticky that says . . . well, what does it say?"

"It says 'ope-u,'" said Sophie.

Eddie was so annoyed, he almost dashed out to say so. He had written it very *clearly* in blueberry juice:

open

"Open," said the New Librarian. "It says 'Open.'"

"Open what?" someone asked.

Curious, the children pushed forward. Within seconds the desk was surrounded. The huge

Squisher legs blocked out the light, causing the area under the desk to grow dark. Alfie backed nervously into the center, making the kind of twitchy movements *you* might make if you were surrounded by titanosaurs.

"Well," said Mr. B, "Sophie found this message stuck to the desk drawer. Right, Sophie?"

"Yes."

"So do you think we should try opening the *drawer*?"

There was a buzz of voices. A pair of sneakers at the front of the crowd ran to the back, accompanied by a shriek.

"Don't be scared," whispered Eddie. "It's just *me*! And blueberry juice."

"Let's give it a try," said the New Librarian. He pulled on the drawer handle. "Stuck."

"Pull harder," said a girl beside the drawer. Eddie liked the sound of *her*.

There was a noisy *scraaawwwkkkk*, and—

"There!" said the Librarian. "It's open. What do you see?"

Eddie held his breath.

"Nothing," said the brave girl. "It's empty."

"Exactly. Does anyone see a ghost in here?"

Silence.

"All right then," said the Librarian. "So that's the end of that."

He started to close the drawer.

"Oh, no," thought Eddie. "Don't!"

Scraawwkk.

"It's stuck," said Sophie. "Again!"

Eddie held his breath. . . .

But Mr. B just laughed and walked away, as if a stuck drawer was the last thing on a busy librarian's mind. "Oh, good!" he said. "Malcolm's found that tape we were looking for. Back to work, everyone."

Eddie couldn't help himself. As the children left, he started leaping about with excitement.

"It's open!" he told Alfie. "The drawer's open!"

Alfie hopped, too. He started to yell, "YAA—"

You will understand, of course, why Eddie had to put a stop to *that*!

When his brother calmed down, Eddie released him and stepped into the open. He stared up at the desk. Remembering his first day in the Library, he half expected to see a small dark head with waving antennae. He could almost hear Min's voice. "Up here, Eddie. Look up!"

But that was then.

"Where's Auntie Min?" asked Alfie. He was as subdued as Eddie had ever seen him. That's when Eddie realized—Alfie was worried, too.

What might they find in the drawer?

"We should wait till the Squishers are gone," said Eddie.

The words were hardly out of his mouth when he changed his mind. "I *can't* wait!" he said. "I just can't!"

"Me NEITHER!" said Alfie. "Let's GO!"

So right then and there, with the Library full of children, the bug brothers attempted a climb. Within seconds, footsteps approached. They scurried back down.

Again, they tried. More thudding footsteps.

On their third try, a child strolled up and leaned
her stomach against the desk—*right beside the
crawling bugs*. She didn't see them. She didn't
touch them. But she was far too close for Eddie.

"We have to wait," he told Alfie.

"AAWWW," said Alfie.

A new group of children arrived—first grade.
It seemed they would *never* leave. Three of them
dawdled at the end, checking
out books. Eddie felt a powerful urge to bite them!

Finally, the Library was empty.

Eddie and Alfie clambered up the desk. They leaped into the open drawer and raced to the back corner.

Aunt Min lay there, curled up and still.

Seeing her, Eddie went cold all over. She looked like . . .

The Spider. She looked just like the Spider the last time Eddie had seen it, propped up against the baseboard. Shriveled. Dry. Dull. Eyes glazed.

"Is Auntie Min DEAD?" asked Alfie in his shrill voice.

"Hush," replied Eddie. He spoke in the gentlest of whispers. "Aunt Min?"

And that was when Alfie lost it. He was, after all, very young, and he could no longer contain himself.

"AUNTIE MIN!" he screeched. "WAKE UP!"

Eddie was about to scold Alfie. But then . . . he thought he saw Min move.

"Do that again," he told his brother.

"AUNTIE MIN! IT'S US! ALFIE AND EDDIE. SAAAY SOMETHING!"

Min stirred weakly. A leg jerked.

"Ooh," she moaned.

"Go get some of that blueberry," Eddie told Alfie. "Run! She loves blueberry, and it's full of juice."

Moments later, the brothers were feeding their aunt fresh blueberry. It was a long time before she could speak.

In the meantime, Alfie talked enough for everyone.

"Everything's OKAY now, Auntie Min. The Grischer is GONE, and the LIBRARY'S SAVED, and we have a NEW LIBRARIAN named MR. B."

"What . . . ," said Min. "What is . . . Mr. B . . . like?"

Alfie answered immediately. "He looks like Eddie."

"Eddie?"

"YES, Auntie Min. He's the very same color of GREEN!"

Min smiled. "Then he must be . . . unusually handsome." She turned to Eddie. "Is everything . . . truly . . . okay?"

This was his chance to tell her the whole story, all the parts she had missed—the buttons, the posters, the parents, the niece, the reporter. It took a long time.

When he finished, Min's eyes were glowing. "You . . . did it," she said slowly. "You . . . saved the Library, Eddie . . . so proud."

Eddie tried to take this in. "Did I? Did I really? Wow, Aunt Min, I can hardly believe it. The stickies worked!"

"They . . . certainly did," said Min. "Excellent . . . writing. Bravo, Eddie!"

CHAPTER
32

In the days that followed, Eddie and Alfie looked after Aunt Min like worker bees tending a queen. They brought her fresh food. They helped her to a spot where she could see sunshine, clouds, and trees through the skylight. They supported her as she began to walk again.

And early one morning right after dawn, they lifted her out of the drawer and onto the pages of an open book.

"What's this?" she cried in delight.

"It's *Anne of Green Gables*," said Eddie. "It was in Miss Cavendish's cabinet, and the New Librarian left it here on the desk last night. Miss Cavendish's niece said it was her favorite book ever—and I remembered that it was one of yours, too."

"Oh, yes!" exclaimed Min. "Anne with an *e*. Always in trouble. Anne is the Squisher I *would* have been if I had been born a Squisher."

She began to walk slowly along the lines, absorbing every word.

"I feel so much better," she said to Eddie when she'd finished.

"Good," said Eddie. "Alfie and I were worried. We thought you were—"

"I know. I came close. I lost hope and sank into a very deep torpor. That's something we bugs can do to survive a bad situation. But we can't do it for long or . . ."

She didn't have to finish her sentence.

"Alfie woke you up," said Eddie.

"Yes, he did," said Min. "Like the prince waking Sleeping Beauty."

"Well," said Eddie, "not *exactly* like that." He pointed at Alfie, who was bouncing on the open book.

"You're right," said Min with a laugh. "Not *exactly.*"

As Eddie and Alfie waited for Min's health to improve, they stayed hidden, as always, during school hours. Eddie was fascinated by all the things children did in the Library, and while Min rested, he and Alfie watched from under the desk. What they saw was probably, to someone like you, perfectly ordinary. But to Eddie, it was new and full of wonder. Finding out about Mars? He couldn't wait. A poetry slam? How amazing! A library scavenger hunt? How he wished he could join in! And when the fourth-grade students wrote e-mails to their favorite characters, Eddie practically swooned. He was *dying* to write to Stuart.

Alfie got fired up, too. He had never shown any interest in reading before, but story time won him over. He especially loved stories that were scary. As he listened to *This Is Not My Hat*, his eyes almost popped out.

"There's a BIG FISH there, Eddie! LOOK! It's FOLLOWING him! Doesn't that little fish SEE?" Hiding behind Eddie, Alfie peeked out alarmed.

Eddie was shocked. Could this be the same Alfie who had run boldly across the Library floor in full view of giant Squishers?

But Alfie was also very fond of fearful characters.

"HAH!" he said, when the Librarian read *Scaredy Squirrel*. "Scaredy's so scared, he doesn't even want to leave his TREE. I never get THAT scared!"

In the end, though, the thing that affected Alfie the most—in fact, it changed his life forever—was kindergarten. One day when the kindergarteners arrived, the New Librarian opened a very big book. It looked as though it was made for giant Squishers. The story was called *Brown Bear, Brown Bear, What Do You See?*, and as the New Librarian read it aloud, he held it so the kindergarteners could see the words. They began to join in.

Watching from under the desk, Alfie figured it out. Those children were learning to *read* with the giant book!

So the next time the kindergarteners read the book out loud—Alfie joined in, too. By the time the bell rang, he was reading. Not a lot. But enough to get him excited. And Alfie excited was like a cloud of singing cicadas.

"I CAN READ, I CAN READ!" he yelled when he joined Min and Eddie in the drawer.

After that, he was desperate to read. So desperate, in fact, that Eddie wrote some words on stickies for him. He made the words smaller this time and used only one foot to write them:

bug

rug

hug

But that wasn't all. Eddie thought very hard about the books he had read and how they were constructed. With this in mind, he wrote the words perpendicular to the glue strip. Each time he finished writing a sticky, he glued it on top of the previous one. He did three stickies that way. Then he put one sticky on backward as a back cover.

"A book!" said Min when he was finished. "You've made a *book*, Eddie. Your first."

"It's only tiny," said Eddie.

"Everyone has to start somewhere," said Min.

Alfie loved his new book. He read it again and again.

On Sunday Min announced that she felt well enough to go home.

"Really? Are you sure?" asked Eddie.

"If I have you and Alfie to help me."

"YAAAAY!" said Alfie.

The hard part was getting off the desk. Aunt Min wasn't heavy now, but she was still very weak and couldn't support herself. Eddie and Alfie had to figure out how to help her while still holding onto the desk themselves. It took all of Eddie's strength, and he could tell by Alfie's grunts that it was just as tough for him.

When they reached the bottom, Min took a moment to rest. She stood there making the same thrumming sound she had made once before—a haunting sound, full of longing and appreciation.

"Oh, I do love this place," she said.

When they reached the doorway, she paused again.

"You did it, Eddie," she said, looking around.

"You saved the Ferny Creek School Library."

Eddie didn't know what to say. He looked around, too, taking in a last sweet breath of paper and ink and stories.

"Can we come BACK for the PARTY?" asked Alfie.

"Absolutely," said Min. "Just try to stop us." Then, leaning on Alfie for support, she stepped out into the hall.

Eddie turned back one last time. "Bye," he whispered to the Library. "Don't go away."

The Library didn't answer. How could it?

But it seemed to breathe a smile as Eddie left.

He felt it on his antennae.

EPILOGUE

When Eddie and Alfie and Min returned home to the crack-in-the-wall, they were greeted with a welcome such as you have never seen. The excitement was incredible! Never since Grandma Ruth's Great Escape from the Glass Tank had there been such a glorious adventure in the family.

For the stay-at-home relatives, the weeks of waiting had been painful. So when all three adventurers walked in, alive and happy, it was almost too much to bear.

"Min! Eddie! Alfie!" came the cries. There was grabbing and hugging and clutching and clinging, and even a bit of crunching as everyone mobbed the arrivals.

"Back now!" hollered Pa finally. "Back off! Give them air, for gosh sake."

"Pa's right," said Ma. "Get back!"

She swatted away a few grubs, and the rest of the family settled down.

Their faces all said the same thing.

Tell!

Please tell us the story of where you have been, and what you have done, and how you have managed to return from the Great Scary World of Outside.

And so began three days of stories.

Yes, it took *that* long.

To keep everyone going, there was a three-day feast. As it happened, there had been a pizza party in the classroom on Friday, with cake for dessert. Pa had led a few brave buglets on a daring raid before the Cleaner came, so there were plenty of bits and pieces to snack on when anyone felt hungry.

"So," said Ma. "Tell us everything."

Well, of course, as you know, there was a great deal to tell—far too much to repeat here. As Min and Eddie and Alfie started to describe their adventures, they realized that between them, they had experienced not one story, but many. Eddie was the one who gave the stories titles, and as you were there for the whole thing, you will probably recognize the titles he made up:

Aunt Min's Terrible Accident
Eddie's Heroic Journey
The Sinister Spider
The Great Page Turn

The Attack of the Killer Mop

The Secret of the Yellow Stickies

The Mysterious Midnight Mouse

The Ghost of Ferny Creek Library

Alfie Rides a Shoe

Actually, you may not recognize that *last* title. Even Eddie and Min didn't recognize it.

"What?" said Eddie when Alfie first mentioned it. "What are you talking about? What shoe?"

"It's how I GOT THERE," said Alfie. "Nobody ever ASKED!"

It was true, Eddie realized. He had never asked. He had always assumed that Alfie had traveled to the Library the same way he did. A long, hard hike. One foot after another after another.

"I'm asking now," said Eddie. "How did you get to the Library?"

"When I got to the classroom DOOR," said Alfie, "it was SCARY! I was all by myself, and I didn't know WHICH way to go! The hall was so BIG!"

"I know," said Eddie. "So what did you do?"

"Nothing," said Alfie. "I just WAITED."

"For what?"

"For some CHILDREN," said Alfie. "And then they came, and they were in a LINE, and they were carrying LIBRARY BOOKS!"

"And then?"

"One of them STOPPED to tie his SHOELACE. So I ran to his other shoelace and used it to crawl up. Onto his SHOE! It was like riding a HORSE, Eddie. Remember that story about COWBOY SMALL? It was like that! I hung onto the shoe-lace, and I RODE THE SHOE—all the way to the LIBRARY!"

Eddie was gobsmacked. So was everyone else. There was a moment of silence, then a cheer broke out from all the little bugs and grubs in the room.

"YAAAAAAAAAAAY!"

Eddie joined in. He couldn't believe he had missed Alfie's shoe story.

"Alfie," he said. "I am sooo happy you followed me."

Ma, of course, had a different reaction to Alfie Rides a Shoe. It was the same reaction she'd had to the Mop, Mouse, and Spider stories.

"Holy Egyptian scarab! What were you *thinking*!"

But she did listen—all the way through. And at the end, she always said the same thing. "Thank heavens that's over, and you're home safe."

Eddie could tell, though, as he watched his mother, that she really *did* love the stories. She shushed anyone who interrupted, which was usually Alfie. And she often asked to have a part repeated. What she loved most were the stories about family. Anybody's family, but especially her own.

Her favorite story, though it never got a title, was how Eddie had rescued Aunt Min from the drawer. After Ma heard that, she walked straight over to Eddie and gave him a hug.

"Oh, my brave little bug," she said proudly, right in front of everyone.

Hearing that, Eddie remembered another

moment, not long before, when he had stood on a book on the story-time carpet and read the following words:

"Oh, my brave little son," said Mrs. Little proudly, as she kissed Stuart and thanked him.

"Thank you, Eddie," said Ma now, with a big smile.

Eddie felt warm all through.

It turned out that everyone had a favorite story. Aunt Min loved The Great Page Turn. When Eddie showed how he had pushed, pushed, pushed to get the page to flop over, she clapped with such excitement that she flopped over sideways herself.

As for the younger bugs, well, most of them were like Alfie. They liked to be scared. They especially enjoyed The Attack of the Killer Mop. Eddie found himself exaggerating some bits, making the tidal wave even bigger than it had been, and the water even filthier. And when he demonstrated his swimming technique, his siblings couldn't stop clapping.

Eddie *loved* telling stories to his family. But he couldn't help wishing they could be written down somewhere, too, so they would last. Like the stories on the shelves of a Library.

"Well, why not?" said Min when he mentioned this longing. "Think of the writing you've done so far."

"Oh, *that* wasn't much," said Eddie. "All I can write is tiny bits."

"A writer's a writer, no matter how small," said Min.

Eddie smiled.

"And besides," said Min. "I think you're forgetting something."

"What?"

"Your favorite word."

"I have a favorite word?"

"Well, you use it in . . . difficult moments. You say it whenever you get into a jam."

"Really?" said Eddie, puzzled.

"Yes, dear. Think about it."

So Eddie did. He thought about the days on his big adventure when things had gotten tough. He thought about times when he'd felt that he just couldn't do it. Too small. Too young. Too dreamy. Too green. He remembered that he had often felt useless or hopeless. He had even felt ready to give up.

"Thank you, Aunt Min," he said, when at last he remembered the word.

He didn't know what would come next. What he might do. Where he could go. What he would read, or write. But as Aunt Min had reminded him, he *did* know a word that would help him on his journey. He had known it all along. Funny, he thought, what a difference a word could make.

The first thing he was going to do when the family celebration was over was find some tools. A yellow sticky. A juicy berry. He would start by writing a message to himself. He would stick it up beside his sleeping place in the crack-in-the-wall, just like a poster in a library. He would read it every day.

His message would be simple.

One word.

try

EDDIE & MIN'S BUGLIOGRAPHY

Alice's Adventures in Wonderland, by Lewis Carroll

Anne of Green Gables, by L. M. Montgomery

The Borrowers, by Mary Norton

Brown Bear, Brown Bear, What Do You See?, written by Bill Martin Jr. and illustrated by Eric Carle

The Cat in the Hat, by Dr. Seuss

Charlie and the Chocolate Factory, by Roald Dahl

Charlotte's Web, by E. B. White

Click, Clack, Moo: Cows That Type, written by Doreen Cronin and illustrated by Betsy Lewin

Cloudy With a Chance of Meatballs, written by Judi Barrett and illustrated by Ron Barrett

Cowboy Small, written and illustrated by Lois Lenski

The Day the Crayons Quit, written by Drew Daywalt, illustrated by Oliver Jeffers

Diary of a Wimpy Kid series, written and

illustrated by Jeff Kinney

Fancy Nancy series, written by Jane O'Connor and illustrated by Robin Preiss Glasser

Harry Potter series, by J. K. Rowling

Horton Hears a Who!, written and illustrated by Dr. Seuss

Lilly's Purple Plastic Purse, written and illustrated by Kevin Henkes

Little Fur Family, written by Margaret Wise Brown and illustrated by Garth Williams

The Nutshell Library, written and illustrated by Maurice Sendak:

> *Chicken Soup with Rice*
>
> *One Was Johnny*
>
> *Pierre*
>
> *Alligators All Around*

Peter and Wendy (also known as *Peter Pan*), written by J. M. Barrie

The Polar Express, written and illustrated by Chris Van Allsburg

Scaredy Squirrel, written and illustrated by Mélanie Watt

Stuart Little, written by E. B. White and illustrated by Garth Williams

The Tale of Peter Rabbit, written and illustrated by Beatrix Potter

This Is Not My Hat, written and illustrated by Jon Klassen

Thomas the Tank Engine, written by Reverend Wilbert Awdry

The Very Hungry Caterpillar, written and illustrated by Eric Carle

Where the Wild Things Are, written and illustrated by Maurice Sendak

Winnie-the-Pooh, written by A. A. Milne and illustrated by Ernest H. Shepard

The Wonderful Wizard of Oz, written by L. Frank Baum

ACKNOWLEDGMENTS

Writing a book about bugs and school libraries, I am grateful to have had expert advice in both areas. Huge thanks to Tess Grainger and Don Griffiths for answering my many questions about bugs. On school library matters, I am deeply appreciative of Janet Mumford and Nancy Hundal, not only for their inspirational work as teacher-librarians, but also for their generous suggestions and advice. Thanks too to Tim Smith for his helpful thoughts on school systems and administration. Any errors, omissions and taking-wild-liberties-for-the-purposes-of-fantasy are entirely my own.

Many thanks also to the following. My fabulous writer pals for feedback, encouragement and/or idyllic island retreats—Deborah Hodge, Norma Charles, Beryl Young, Susin Nielsen, Margriet Ruurs, Ainslie Manson, Ellen McGinn, and everyone, past and present, in the PB group. My excellent agent, Hilary McMahon, for finding such fine publishing homes for *Tiny Hero*. My ever-so-wise editors for their insights and valuable ideas—Virginia Duncan at Greenwillow Books and Tara Walker at Tundra Books. And of course, Lia, Tess, and Maurice, who *always* laugh when they're supposed to.